OOPS!

Darrell Bain's Latest
Collection of Short Stories

Introduction
By
Jim Brown

OOPS! Darrell Bain's Latest Collection of Short Stories

ISBN: 978-1905091-72-0
Paperback version

Published by LL-Publications © 2010
www.ll-publications.com
57 Blair Avenue
Hurlford
Scotland
KA1 5AZ

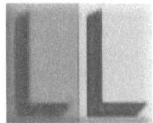

Edited by Jim Brown
Book layout and typesetting by jimandzetta.com
Cover concept by Darrell Bain
Cover Design by Helen E. H. Madden © LL-Publications 2010

Printed in the UK and the USA
Published in paperback and digital formats

Publishing credits:

Cure for an Ailing Alien & Retribution
previously published by LL-Publications 2009

A Simple Idea
Coyote Scare
OOPS!
Robyn's Rock
A Steel Trap Mind
The Furniture Formula
Golden Years
Why Read an Ebook on Your Computer
PSI Ability?
Another Furniture Formula
Math Madness
The Naughty Bed
Samantha's Talent
previously published by Double Dragon Ebooks 2006-2008

INTRODUCTION by Jim Brown

Darrell Bain first came to my attention when I joined the industry group, EPIC, several years ago. He had been looking for a publisher to put one of his eBooks into print. Seeing the credits that Darrell had – even at that time – I offered to consider his book. That book was *Bark!* – the tale of a little dog who could spot alien shape-shifters. This was no children's book, but it was one of the funniest, and creative books I'd ever read, and Darrell Bain had me hooked.

You could say Darrell Bain is a man of many talents. He's served in Vietnam, and he's been a Christmas tree farmer in Texas. He worked for many years in the medical field in surgery, pharmacy and laboratory, and has a degree in Medical Technology. Now he's a highly regarded award-winning author. He took up writing full-time when he retired from Christmas tree farming, and his first book, *Medics Wild*, was a fictional story based on his armed forces service in Vietnam with his two brothers. He's now the author of over fifty books.

Awards were to follow quickly: **Knowbetter best Science Fiction Novel, 2003**, for *The Sex Gates;* **Fictionwise Author of the Year, 2005**; Multiple **Epic Awards** for **Best Adventure/Adventure** and **Young Adult Novels**; Multiple **Epic finalist** for **Best Science Fiction Novel;**

Multiple **Dream Realm Awards** for **Best Science Fiction Novels.**

So what makes Darrell Bain write so well? Sometimes that answer lies with readers and not the writer himself, or the publisher. But as an avid reader as well as a publisher, let me tell you what the reader in me sees:

In much the same way as the compelling narrative tones of James Earl Jones will convey the spoken word to you in an easy, effortless tone, so the writing style of Darrell Bain will convey a story to you through easy prose. There's little that complicates Darrell's writing, but don't let that fool you. His imagination and wonderful creativity can take what appears to be a simple story-line and magnetize it, pulling you in – often with many smiles or chuckles (although he doesn't really regard himself as a comedy writer). His numerous awards are a testament to this remarkable ability to see a story in the most innocent of everyday occurrences.

Bark! is a great example of this. Darrell's own very quirky little dachshund, Tonto, plus the backdrop of his own Christmas tree farm, became the inspirations behind the story. Adding to the mix, and pivotal to the plot, was the ingredient of Darrell's own frustrations at government and politicians. The result was a sci-fi tale of an ADHD afflicted little dog who turns out to be the only thing that can save the planet from an accidental invasion of aliens – not to mention incompetent politicians!

In this collection, *OOPS!*, Darrell has inserted little intros and afterthoughts to most of the stories, which gives a very fascinating insight into how the mind of a great storyteller works.

That's what Darrell Bain is – a *great* storyteller.

CONTENTS

I'm sure I'm not the only person who makes a habit of complaining about the idiocy, corruption and entirely self-serving hooligans we keep electing to office in this great United States of America but I wonder how many others have actively tried to devise a system in their own minds for eliminating such people from office? I did that one time for a few days and this story is what came of it.

A SIMPLE IDEA

Johnny Trevane tried to take in all of William Despetit's image while still keeping his father and mother and little brother in sight. The holodigital statue was magnificent. It was huge, bigger than any of the others he had ever seen, the largest of any in the known worlds. It was splendid; a grand awe-inspiring sight that almost took his breath away, despite having been told in advance how marvelous it was. The enlarged reproduction of William Despetit stood with one leg slightly forward, looking into the far distance with his lips curved into a hint of a smile, as if satisfied with the universe and mankind's place in it. One arm hung naturally and gracefully at his side. The other was raised, bent at the elbow in order to support an opened book.

Johnny remembered to breathe again. He puffed his cheeks as he blew out stale air and adjusted his head band again so the audio stayed in the background. It was getting too small for him, he thought, or maybe he just needed a haircut. He scanned Mister Despetit's likeness one more time then ... *Dad! Mom!* Where were they? Where was Kevin, the brat? He looked frantically into the throng walking past him from the interior of the spaceport and out into the covered concourse where slideways carried them along, splitting into narrower ways that branched and branched again. How could they have gotten so far ahead of him so quickly? Or were they? It was hard to tell with so many taller adults around. He ran forward the few steps to where the slideway split then stopped. Which way? What if he took the slideway to the right and they had gone left? He felt the first hint of panic intruding into his mind.

"Young man, could I help you? You look as though you might have misplaced your family."

Johnny glanced up at the plain, honest face of the stranger. Age lines managed to fit comfortably with his graying hair, giving him a grandfatherly appearance, though with a hint of sadness about it. But it was sort of nice, Johnny thought, the man trying to make a joke of him being lost. Dad probably wouldn't think it was funny, though. Nor Mom either, and the brat would laugh and laugh. "Yes, sir, I guess I hid them a little too well."

"I'm Fred McIntyre. Come on, let's go over to the customer service counter and see what they can do for you. What's your name, by the way, so they'll know who the lost people are?"

"Johnny Trevane, sir," he answered as he followed his new friend along to the slidewalk. He gave no thought at all to the possibility that a stranger in a strange city on a strange planet might do him harm. Things like that were mostly unheard of anywhere outside history books. Which reminded him; he wanted another book on the North American continent, where they would be living for the next year. The first one hadn't had much depth; it was more for pre-schoolers than primary citizens, he thought.

The service counter was located only a few seconds along the 'way, on a branch ending in a cul-de-sac. "Hello," Mr. McIntyre said to the young lady, an intern by the look of her white blouse and dark blue skirt. "There should be an inquiry shortly concerning some lost parents by the name of Trevane. Would you mind letting us know when they turn up?"

"Certainly sir. Where will you be?"

"We're going to sit over on the benches with the other folks that're waiting for lost companions." He produced a data cube and slid it across the counter. The young lady took it for a moment and fitted it into the reader. Her eyes widened slightly as she handed it back to Mr. McIntyre. He smiled genially at her. "Would it be possible to have some coffee while we're waiting?"

"Certainly, sir. Just have a seat and the bench will take care of you. There's reading material as well, if you like."

"Thanks. You're very helpful."

The girl blushed and nodded.

"You do drink coffee, don't you?" Mr. McIntyre asked Johnny as he led the way to the cluster of padded, comfortable benches where several other adults and children of various ages waited.

"Yes, sir. Thank you. With cream if they have it. But will we have time to finish? I'd hate for you to waste your credit if my parents show up soon."

"It'll be a while. They'll have to take the slideway several turns before they can get off and find one coming back, especially if they're not familiar with Earthport, which I assume they aren't."

"That's right. My Dad was born on earth, but he hasn't been back since way before he and Mom were married. The rest of us are Santellians. Dad came back to do some advanced micromagnetic studies so he can upgrade the planetary com links back home."

"That's a good planet, so I hear. Still not crowded and lots of opportunity for service."

"I'm going to be a teacher," Johnny stated with the certainty of the young, although in his case he had been inclined toward teaching ever since entering primary citizenship after finishing pre-school.

"That's a fine profession. A very fine profession. I saw you admiring Mr. Despetit. I assume you took a little too long at it?"

Johnny thought he might be blushing. He hoped not. "I guess maybe I did, but ... it's such a grand image. I wonder why so many people couldn't read before he came along?"

Mr. McIntyre glanced at his thumb watch and decided there was time for a discussion with the youngster. "Well, it's not so much that they couldn't read as that they wouldn't. They seemed to think there were too many other, more interesting ways to occupy their time. Or have you gotten that far along in your history yet?"

Johnny gave a guilty little smile at the adult. "I guess I sort of peek ahead when I should be doing regular lessons and assigned reading. Dad says one of these days I'm going to forget how many books I have going and miss a regular lesson.

And he thinks it's a bad example for the br ... for my little brother."

Mr. McIntyre winked at him. "I did the same thing when I was your age. It won't hurt you, I don't think. Why, look at me; I made a good living before I retired and I always got ahead of myself."

"What did you do, sir?"

"Oh, I helped run the government. One of those pesky jobs that aren't very interesting but necessary. Governments are always necessary, but I'm glad we've got it down to a bare minimum, most places now. In the olden days, some countries had as many as one service employee for every dozen or so inhabitants."

"*Really*? Gosh, that's hard to believe. Why that would make..." he did some mental calculations and frowned. "...it would make it impossible to hold up over the long term. Wouldn't it?" He looked anxiously at the grownup, thinking he must have made a mistake somewhere.

"No, your calculations are right. Such ratios are unsustainable in the long run, which is why all the old systems never lasted. It took a man like William Despetit to figure out a way of governing ourselves that really worked."

"It seems so simple," Johnny mused. "And all the materials were right there. How come it took so long to get started? Centuries!"

"More like Millennia. A couple of them anyway. But sometimes the simple ideas and what seems in retrospect the most obvious ones are sometimes the hardest to discover and implement. For instance, do you think Mr. Despetit could have put his idea across without the discovery of cerebrosocioimaging technology and inexpensive digital recording so the economically deprived could afford to participate?"

Johnny scratched his head. "Well ... I guess there would have been lots of cheating without the CSI scope." The mere thought of someone cheating or lying about such basic requirements seemed outright foreign to him but apparently such things had happened in the past since he'd read about them in his histories.

"No doubt about it. In fact there would have been so many ways to get around the requirements that the idea almost certainly would have failed. As it is though, we have the most stable, efficient and just government in history. To be fair about it though, there's a few other ideas which might—notice I say might—have worked almost as well."

"Really?"

"Sure. Ever read any science fiction, the old masters?"

Johnny's expression brightened like a flower unfolding. "Oh! I remember now. *Heinlein! Starship Troopers*! Where a person had to serve in the military before they could vote. Would that have really produced a good government? I never could decide."

McIntyre shrugged. "It might have, but since it was never tried, we'll never know."

"Anyway, we don't have wars now," Johnny said.

McIntyre sipped at his coffee the bench end table had produced. "It's a big universe. We still may meet our equal—or even our superior—in space. I think our system would serve just as well if that ever happens. We have far, far more potential candidates for military service than we'd need, I think. But let's get back to how our system got started. Have you read much about it?"

"Yes, sir. It's real interesting, how William Despetit started out and convinced one city in one of the old … states?"

"Yes, states. A political subdivision, like a county or city."

"Anyway, I've read a primary book about it but I'd like to get some more if I can sneak them out of Dad's library." Johnny was talking so easily and casually to Mr. McIntyre that he completely forgot he was confessing to pilfering book downloads from his father. It wasn't often he had such an interesting conversation with an adult. "He got one city started and it worked so well that a few more imitated him. Then it went on to … county, you said?"

"Right. One step up from a city."

"So once he proved it worked in cities and counties, more and more of them began to do the same thing, and then it got going at the state level. That's when the persons who were in power from national elections without Mr. Despetit's requirements got worried his system would be made mandatory in order to run for office. And that's when the fighting started, I guess."

"Right you are. I think that must have been a better book than you let on." McIntyre was enjoying himself. The youngster was obviously brighter than normal and read a great deal, far more than the basic requirements for primary citizenship.

Johnny saw the old man was taking pleasure in his display of knowledge. He continued, not trying to show off but simply enjoying himself. "The other side almost won, too, except they didn't have as much financial power as Mr. Despetit's backers did. I guess a lot of people were killed before the whole nation went over to his system."

"There were, indeed, but history says it was justified, don't you think?"

Johnny was stumped there. "Sir, I don't know about that, killing and all. Maybe if they had gone slower it wouldn't have been necessary."

A bright lad, indeed. "Perhaps. But you have to remember that the nation where it began—right here on the North American continent—wasn't existing in isolation. Its economy was intermingled with that of the rest of the world. Had the civil war lasted very long, other nations might have intervened and suppressed our system in order to stabilize the economic flow of goods, services and money. Had that happened ... well, we might not even have space travel or some of the other developments which followed after other nations began seeing how well the system worked in North America and began adopting it, too."

"Gosh. All that for an idea so simple."

McIntyre glanced up and past Johnny's head. He saw a middle-aged man and woman standing and listening. The woman was holding a very sleepy young boy. He winked at the family, knowing who they must be but they were apparently content to wait for the inadvertent history lesson being given to their son to play out to the end.

"Yes, it was simple, but even after it went into effect over most of the world, there was still intense debate and political, if not military, fighting."

"What for, once it was in?"

"Well, today the questions are all settled but back then they weren't. For instance, how long must the books be? On what subjects, if any? Should some subjects be mandatory? What sort of age limit to place on eligibility for service? Indeed, what sort of services should we have at all? The system couldn't exist in a vacuum. Then there were the ones who got into government then tried to change the system afterward. That caused lots of dissent, and some rather violent protests even got out of hand. But it all worked out in the end, and it's constantly monitored today for improvements and in order to prevent recidivism."

"I guess I'll learn all that later on."

McIntyre shrugged and again winked at the couple standing slightly behind and to the right of them. "There's no reason you can't read about it now if you feel you're up to the advanced texts. Are you?"

"Golly, yes. It's all so interesting! Maybe I'll teach about it when I'm grown."

"Now wouldn't that be fine? Combining your career with a prime interest? Personally, I think that's the best combination possible. It's what I did when I was getting started and I kept at it until I retired."

At that moment, Johnny caught sight of a familiar figure from the corner of his eye. He turned toward it. *Mom! Dad! Where have you been?*

Mr. Trevane tried to look grim with only moderate success. "It's more like where you've been, young man. Didn't I tell you not to get separated from us?"

"Yes, sir. I guess I was looking at the image of Mr. Despetit too long."

"Well, I can sort of understand that," the older Trevane relented, remembering the first time he had stood before the image of the great man. "There's no figure in history more important."

"My feelings exactly," McIntyre said as he stood.

Johnny's father shook McIntyre's hand. "John Trevane, Senior. I'm honored to meet you sir, and I thank you for watching Johnnie until we could find our way back here."

"No problem at all. We were enjoying ourselves, talking about the requirements for public service and how the system got started."

"Johnnie ought to already know everything about it, as much as he reads, and as many times as he's downloaded books from my library without asking."

The younger Trevane's mouth dropped open. *Dad had known all along!*

McIntyre laughed. "Too bad he can't count those in the ten books a month requirement, isn't it?"

"It doesn't matter. He's always way ahead, though sometimes he does have to jump to keep up the non-fiction requirement. He enjoys fiction so much."

"I like history, too, Dad," Johnnie proclaimed. "Mr. McIntyre was telling me all about the troubles the ten book a month reading obligation for citizenship had when it first got started. I'm going to teach about it when I get my certification."

"That's fine, son. I have some fiction describing those days, too, if you'd like to borrow them."

"Yes, sir!"

"Thanks again, Mr. McIntyre. We really do have to get going or we'll miss our connections."

"It was my pleasure. Have a nice trip and take care of this young man. I have a feeling we'll be hearing from him in years to come."

McIntyre went on his way, thinking back over his career and how much he had enjoyed it. Government service was a real pleasure these days, though somewhat boring. Like the young lad had said, such a simple idea. One must read and comprehend at least six fiction and four non-fiction books a month before being eligible to run for public office, be a constable, serve in the military or work in any of the other branches of government. The reading had to continue, of course, with cerebrosocioimaging technology to make certain the eligibility requirements were met and kept while serving. Such a simple idea, but such an effective one. In the olden days no one really knew what made a person a reader or non-reader, but the statistics were reliable. On average, those who had the reading habit, in both fiction and non-fiction, almost automatically made good citizens and good public servants. That was Despetit's discovery, and today of course, it was well known how the reading habit gradually rewired the brain into constructive pathways. Pre-schoolers were all exposed to the method right from the start and for the vast majority, it took. Yes, such a simple idea, but it had certainly changed the old world—and now the system was spreading to the stars.

"Son, do you know who you were talking to?"

"Sure. He told you his name. Didn't you hear it? Fred McIntyre."

"Uh huh. The same Fred McIntyre who was the last president of earth. A real statesman. You should be pleased he took the time to talk to you."

"Gosh! I am, Dad! Wow!" Johnny reflected for a moment. "You know, Dad, he looked a little sad, didn't he?"

"Come to think of it, he did. I wonder why?"

Fred McIntyre walked idly along the slideway leading to the exit he wanted. He wasn't in the least bit of a hurry. He just wished there was more to do in government these days. The ten book system worked so well there wasn't much left of it, other than basic services, and they practically ran themselves. Well, it was a big universe. Young Trevane might find something more interesting out on the frontiers of the new worlds being opened up. He brightened at the thought, then frowned in concentration. *New worlds*. Hell, he wasn't that old. Out where folks were busy taming the planets there ought to be a spot for an old retired politician, and certainly reading his minimum of ten books a month would be no problem. Almost everyone did that anyway, whether they intended to enter public service or not.

He made up his mind with characteristic swiftness. So long as there were books to read and thoughts to think, there would be something for him to do out on the far frontiers. Perhaps if he lived long enough, he'd meet young Trevane as a grown man. He smiled at the thought and was whistling as he took the slideway to the immigration office. As he waited to be taken care of, he pulled out his reader, just as most of the others in the room had done. He was engrossed with the latest edition of *Politics of the Frontier Worlds* when his name was called

The End

I don't know if this idea would work or not, any more than whether Heinlein's requirement of military service for citizenship and voting rights would. It is fun thinking about it, though!

Being married to a nurse makes me wonder why it took me so long to come up with a story like this one and I can't remember now what made it pop into my mind, almost fully plotted.

CURE FOR AN AILING ALIEN

"Are you serious?"

Joanne Levy sat in her favorite chair in the living room of her cozy little home in the Arlington, Virginia suburbs. The place was really too expensive for her income level but a trust left by her grandfather allowed her live there and also to pick and choose her cases. Intensive Care nurses like her, who worked in homes, were scarce and much sought after by the elite of Washington who were ill but despised hospitals. She stared at her visitor and wondered if he was really who he said he was. If so, this case would certainly be the highlight of her career!

"Yes, we're perfectly serious, Ms. Levy. We need a nurse for an alien and you fit our selection criteria. You're single, you're very knowledgeable in your field and you already have a secret clearance." Terrell Jenson, the man sitting across from her spoke in a level tone of voice, but his face bore tension lines from continuous worry.

"But ... I don't know anything about aliens! Good Lord, I didn't even know we were in contact with any until you came here. How could I even start caring for it without the least idea of its bodily functions, its vital signs, its ... oh hell, there's a dozen reasons why not." She felt her pulse rate increase even as she denied having the expertise needed for such a case. *An alien!* She had dreamed of going into space as a young woman. In fact, lately she had been seriously considering spending the money for an orbital trip on one of the privately owned spaceships that were available now, but she was still hesitant. The cost would take a significant bite out of her trust fund.

Jenson eyed her classically pretty profile and long blond hair, picturing her attending the alien with it tied in a bundle behind her neck. The aliens were furry creatures and the one saying it needed medical attention had coloring not far removed from her hair.

"You'd be perfect for the job, Ms. Levy, so please don't worry. I don't think it will ask you to perform surgery or anything really drastic."

"No? Then what would I be doing?"

He shrugged and spread his hands. "I don't know."

"Then I'm sorry. It's an intriguing offer and God knows I've thought and read enough about aliens to want the job, but I'd feel like I was operating under false pretenses. Don't you even have a clue?" Joanne felt horrible about not being able to take the case. She wondered where the alien was now. On earth? In orbit about the planet in its spaceship? He hadn't said.

Jenson considered the situation before he released a bit of knowledge. "Ms. Levy, there is one thing I can tell you. The alien asked specifically for a nurse even after we offered to bring in the most renowned and knowledgeable physicians on earth, of whatever specialty it chose."

"Why? I mean why a nurse but not a doctor."

Jenson granted her a thin smile. "We asked him—it's a *he*, by the way—the same question. The best we were able to interpret its answer is that he refused to subject such learned men or women to failure in case they couldn't help."

Joanne frowned. "Now isn't that strange? But he wouldn't mind a lowly nurse failing. That's not very complimentary."

"No, I suppose it isn't, but ... Ms. Levy, may I trouble you for something to drink while we're talking?"

"Oh! Certainly. And please call me Joanne; I don't like formality that much. Forgive me for not offering you anything before now. When you rang my doorbell and said you were from DARPA, and wanted to talk to me about aliens, my mind went off on a tangent. What would you like?"

Jenson had done his research. He already knew his host favored scotch, so that's what he asked for. And there was method to his request. He hoped she would join him in a couple of drinks herself and perhaps that would loosen her judgment enough to take the job. It certainly couldn't hurt and he really wanted a drink himself.

"I'd like some scotch over ice if you have it, please," he said.

"No problem. I'll be right back."

Jenson watched her leave for the kitchen. The gentle sway of her hips and her slim figure presented an attractive picture. He knew he would have to be careful if he talked her into taking the job. She was single, just as he was, and had no significant other at the moment, also just like him. A romance while undertaking a mission this important risked blurring his concentration while attempting to establish a working relationship with the alien. As yet, he had no idea if it could even be accomplished. In fact, it might very well hinge on the very issue being discussed with Ms—with Joanne right now.

Some of his superiors at DARPA wanted to bring in the state department but he was adamant. He'd dealt with them before. If anyone could foul up the first contact with an alien species it would be either State or the politicians. So far he was able to call the shots. For some unknown reason the alien had picked him as his liaison and refused to talk with anyone else after the initial contact.

"Here you are," Joanne said.

He took the drink from her. This time she sat down on the couch with him. He took it as a sign she was wavering. Perhaps she would relent.

She sipped at her scotch with furrowed brow, then looked at Jenson.

"You do know how wild this sounds, don't you? I still can't help but feel I'm the butt of some elaborate practical joke."

"I know the feeling, Joanne. It was the same way with me when we were first contacted. And by the way, my first name is Terrell."

"How did they contact us? And you keep saying 'alien'. Don't they have a name?"

"Not as a species, apparently. They do have individual designations. The one who wants a nurse is called Shuft. As for how we were contacted ... I'm sorry, but there are some things I can't divulge. I can tell you that this alien is presently on earth."

"Too bad. A space trip might have convinced me."

"Really? Then suppose I guarantee you a three-day orbital trip into space as part of your pay?"

She realized her mouth was hanging open and quickly closed it. "Are you serious? I seem to keep saying that, don't I, Terrell?"

He laughed. "No reason why you shouldn't, especially since the public isn't aware of our contact with them. I'm rather surprised you believed me so easily."

"I guess you've been so serious it's hard not to believe you. And your credentials looked authentic. Besides, no one I know would use DARPA in a joke. Most of them have no idea of what it is or that it even exists."

"All too true. Sad, isn't it?"

"Yes. Tell me one more time now: why me and not someone else?"

"We've talked to other nurses. You're the one we want."

"But why?"

"Perhaps because you admit up front you have no idea how to treat an alien. A couple of others jumped at the chance just to meet an alien and never worried about anything else. Some didn't believe. We wanted a single nurse, and female since that's how our linguist presented the term originally. You're also extremely competent. Not that we think it will make much difference in what you do, but we do want to give the alien our best shot. And who knows? Maybe you'll spot what's wrong with him immediately."

"Not much chance of that. Another drink?"

"Sure."

Jenson was correct in his reasoning. By the time Joanne finished her second scotch rocks she found herself saying the hell with it. Why not? It wasn't as if she hadn't told Terrell she had less idea of how to treat an alien than she did of how to cure halitosis in a walrus.

"I guess if you want me that bad, I'll do my best. But I still can't imagine why they're insisting on a nurse instead of a doctor."

Jenson shrugged. "Just chalk it up to them being alien. That's all we can do. We hardly understand them at all, but it appears they've been studying us pretty thoroughly for quite a while."

"Have they said why they don't have the equivalent of a doctor with them?"

"I asked. The answer didn't make a bit of sense to me but I could tell they didn't want to be pushed on the subject any longer so I let it drop."

Joanne sighed. "All right. When do you want me?"

"How about tomorrow morning at eight?'

"Okay. When do I see the alien?"

"About an hour later."

Joanne fidgeted as the time approached for Jenson to pick her up. She had checked and re-checked her medical kit until she knew its contents by heart. She went over everything he'd told her again and again until she realized she was beating a dead horse. Jenson didn't know and she didn't know what her function would be, but she was almost certain of one thing: her medical kit and the drugs and instruments it included would be useless. She wouldn't dare give it a pill or a shot without knowing how it might affect its metabolism. She had never felt so helpless in her life, and yet ... she was more than anxious to get on with it. *An alien!* The dream of a lifetime!

What would it look like? How would it act? Would ... the doorbell rang. She took a deep breath and steadied herself. She picked up her bag and went to the door. Just before she opened it, an outrageous thought occurred to her. It took all her will power not to burst out laughing in Jenson's face as she considered it.

"Good morning, Joanne. You look well, and very nice in your nurse's outfit, too."

"Thank you, Terrell. You didn't tell me how to dress so I took it upon myself to wear the traditional white uniform. She reached up and touched the unfamiliar garment on her head. "They've gone out of style but I even wore my cap."

"I think you did well. If you're ready, we'll be on our way."

"I'm as ready as I'll ever be," she said, even though butterflies were fluttering inside her. She made an effort and stilled her nervousness as she walked with Jenson to his car.

The nervousness returned, along with more butterflies than ever once they arrived at the DARPA building in the trendy Clarendon neighborhood. Inside, Jenson led her through the lobby and on past the security checkpoint and down a long hall with hardly a pause. Apparently arrangements had already been made. She was expected. The thought made her more jumpy than ever. Eventually they stopped of an unmarked door.

"This is where I leave you, Joanne. Shuft is waiting inside."

He smiled at her and Joanne suddenly realized he was fully as nervous as her. Somehow, the thought that Jenson was uneasy helped to bring her own attitude to a professional level.

"I'm ready." She turned the knob, opened the door and stepped inside.

The last of her residual anxiety evaporated at the sight of the alien. He was humanoid in form and sported long silky hair the color of butterscotch, but what drew her were the eyes. The large orange ovals looked at her in a manner that emanated trust as he rose to his feet.

"Greetings," he said.

"Hello," Joanne responded, then before she could stop, an exclamation burst out of her. "Why you're beautiful!" Unfortunately, as soon as she realized what she'd said, embarrassment suffused her features. What an unprofessional way to begin an examination!

The creature seemed not to mind. "I am Shuft," he said. "I presume you are the nurse I requested?"

"Yes, Mr. Shuft. My name is Joanne Levy, but please call me Joanne. And please sit down"

"Thank you, I shall."

After Shuft was seated again, Joanne said "You requested a nurse so I presume you're feeling unwell. Is that right?"

"Yes, Joanne."

"Since I don't know the vital signs of your species, I believe the best way to begin is simply to ask you some questions. First, are you in pain?"

"Yes."

"Is it localized? Can you show me where you hurt?"

"No, it is a general feeling of unease."

"All right then, on a scale of—wait, do you understand our numerical system?"

"Yes."

"Very well, then. On a scale of one to ten, can you tell me how bad the pain is?"

"It would be about a three or possibly four, depending on the time of day."

"Is it worse at certain times?"

"Yes, it..."

She continued with a stream of questions, asked in her quiet but forceful manner as she tried to get a handle on what was bothering her patient. When the questions ran out, she asked "Do you mind if I examine you?"

"No, not at all."

"Good. Will you stretch out on your bed then, on your back?"

"Certainly."

Joanne had no idea of what she was looking for. She was merely going through the motions, knowing that sometimes the simple laying on of hands was part of the treatment, and sometimes even the cure, of human patients. The high point of the exam came when she touched his head. As she looked into his big trusting eyes she found herself stroking his brow, sleek with the butterscotch hair that covered his body although it wasn't as long on his face as elsewhere. And as she stroked the being, the same outrageous thought she'd had at the doorway of her home came back to her. Somehow it began to seem not quite so extreme.

She had to almost force herself to remove her hand from Shuft's brow. "You may sit up again," she said.

"Thank You. Have you reached any conclusions?"

"Not yet. I notice that you seem to have no problems breathing our atmosphere. How about ... no, let me rephrase that. Do you have any idea whether the microorganisms of our planet can cause you illness?"

"There is no chance of that. Although our bodies can assimilate your food and drink, the infective organisms of earth have no effect on us at all."

"How about our medicines? Our analgesics, the pain relievers. Would they work on your metabolism?"

"I'm afraid not. Our bodies simply neutralize drugs they have not been attuned to."

Again that silly thought. She couldn't get it out of her head. Did she dare? Well, she certainly knew of nothing else that might work. "Mr. Shuft, would it be possible for me to consult with a colleague, then return to see you?"

"Certainly. Whatever you can do to make me feel better would be greatly appreciated."

"Then I think I may have just the thing for you, but I need to talk to someone first. Unfortunately, I don't have it with me, but I can return with it in a few hours."

"That would be fine."

'Thank you Mr. Shuft. It's been a pleasure meeting you and it will give me even more pleasure when I'm able to help you. I'll return shortly."

"Thank you."

"So how did it go?" Terrell asked immediately after Joanne closed the door to the alien's room."

"It went okay, but I'm not finished."

"What else do you need?"

"I'll tell you when we get outside."

She checked her watch once they were back in front of the DARPA building. Amazingly, she found that she had been with the alien for less than an hour. It had seemed like much longer than that. She stopped and turned to Jenson. "Terrell, I need a little privacy while I make a phone call. Okay?"

He shrugged. "Sure." He walked far enough away so that he was out of hearing.

Joanne quickly dialed a number. She spoke for a couple of minutes, then put her phone away and motioned to Jenson.

"Terrell, I need you to drive me somewhere, then bring me back here."

His countenance grew a puzzled expression. "What is it? Where? What—"

She held up her hand. "It's part of the treatment of Shuft."

"Okay, let's go."

They got into his car and she gave him directions. A half hour later they pulled into the driveway of a snug little home in a residential neighborhood.

"Wait here. I won't be but a minute."

"Okay, but you've sure got me intrigued."

She smiled but said nothing. She went to the door and rang the bell. When it opened she stepped inside. She stayed for a few moments then came back out. She was carrying something in a brown paper bag.

Once they were on the way back to DARPA, he asked "What's in the bag?"

"Something for Shuft. Hopefully, a cure."

"Really? What is it?"

"Later. Let's see how it works." She was afraid if she told him what she had, he would refuse to proceed. Probably he would howl with laughter then go find another nurse.

Joanne delivered her package and stayed to visit for a while with Shuft, assuring him all the while that if he followed her advice, he would certainly begin feeling better soon. She smoothed his brow one more time before she left.

Outside again, Jenson said "I see you left your package with Shuft. Can you tell me now what it was?"

"Not yet. If Shuft cares to inform you, I have no objections, but I believe he will feel better if left alone for a while. That's the last thing I told him."

"I'm dying of curiosity."

She laughed. "You'll just have to die. Or would a drink perhaps keep you breathing?"

"Well..."

"Come on in when you get me home. I'll have one, too. This has been a trying day."

"I'm sure it has!"

Joanne answered the doorbell the next day. Terrell had called and said he wanted to come over.

"Hi! Come on in," she said when she opened the door and saw that it was indeed him.

Now it was her turn to be unbearably curious, not him. She had heard nothing about Shuft since she left his presence the previous day and it was getting on toward evening now.

Terrell was on a mission. Before he even sat down, he glared at her. "All right, I give up. You cured Shuft. Completely. Now will you tell me what you used? What you had in that package?"

"He's really cured? No fooling?"

"No fooling. In fact he sends his regards and thanks and wanted me to tell you how appreciative he is of your efforts on his behalf. He says he feels better now than he has in a long while. So what did you use? What was in that damned bag?"

"You're sure you want to know?"

"*Yes*, I want to know! Desperately!"

"Maybe you'd better sit down first."

Terrell screwed up his face in frustration but did so, then gazed at her imploringly.

"My last name didn't give it away?" Joanne asked.

"Your last name? What has that to do with it?"

"Levy. It's a Jewish name."

"So?"

Joanne giggled. She couldn't help it. "You know where we went yesterday? That was my mother's house."

"I guess I'm dumb. I still don't get it."

"What do Jewish mothers always prescribe for sick people?"

Terrell thought for a moment then his mouth dropped open. "You didn't!"

"Yes I did."

"I don't believe it."

"You may as well because that's exactly what I did. I gave him a bowl of my mother's chicken soup and a little reassurance."

"*Chicken soup?* Oh my God! Chicken soup..." His mouth quivered as the words trailed off. His body shook but finally he could hold it in no longer. Laughter exploded from him like a twenty gun salvo from a battleship.

"Chicken soup! Oh my! Chicken soup! Just wait until the folks hear about this one! Chicken soup to cure an alien!"

"Well it worked, didn't it?"

"Yes, but ... never mind. When do you want that trip into space?"

Joanne smiled. "Just as soon as you can go with me."

And they lived happily ever afterwards.

The End

This story brought a lot of chuckles and laughter to readers. Even my editor said he laughed. However ... who knows? Maybe chicken soup really is a cure for everything!

We live in the country on a road named Santa Claus Lane. Really. The Post Office gave it to us when they needed names for all private roads for the 911 service. In my book, Life On Santa Claus Lane, *I said that strange things seemed to happen on our road. One day I got to thinking about some of them. Once I had been scared silly by a coyote on the farm. Several times Betty and I had admired a really beautiful one that happened to cross the edge of our yard. Thinking of the contrast begat a story, the only horror story I've ever written.*

COYOTE SCARE

My wife inherited the hundred acres in the Piney Woods of east Texas from her previous husband, who died at a young age from a heart attack. We had been married a few years and were in our early thirties when we decided to put the land to use by starting a Christmas tree farm. That may sound like a strange decision for a nurse and medical technologist, who may have been born on farms, but hadn't lived on one since they were kids. And it was. A strange decision, I mean. I'm the one who talked my wife into it. I never did have much common sense.

I don't have much mechanical talent, either. No, that's not right. I have no talent for machinery at all, as anyone who's read my books about farm life already knows. Nevertheless, I jumped into farming and carried Hannah along with me, willy nilly. I made a hash of it for years before deciding I'd be much happier and the tractors and trucks and sprayers and mowers and all those other things containing moving parts would be happier, too, if I just wrote about farming instead of actually doing it anymore, but something happened before I could quit and go look for a real job.

Before I retired those blasted tractors, which I swear were sentient and spent the nights conniving with each other about what kind of trouble they would get me into and how much blood they could make me shed the next day, I had an awful experience on one. It had nothing to do with any of the tractor's moving parts, those that spent their time lying in wait for me to come close enough to get bitten or chewed or gouged or gnawed on. Tractors are savage and evil and should be sold with guards whose duty is to threaten them with both barrels of a twelve gauge shotgun the minute they get out of line. Unfortunately, they don't, and one day the tractor decided to take me down to the bottom of a hill where one section of trees was planted. I swear I hadn't intended to work those trees that day; the tractor just drove me there before I realized what was happening. And that's when the trouble started. Trouble? No, that's when the scary stuff started.

Back when I was still farming, most of the acreage not planted in Christmas trees was still wild, with a lot of second growth interspersed with huge old oak trees. With only twenty acres planted in trees and the surrounding land unoccupied, there was lots of room for varmints and animals to roam. We had deer, wildcats, rabbits for the wildcats to chase, raccoons, opossums and foxes. There were huge old gators down in the cypress break at the back of the farm that turned into a swamp if you went very far into it. There were claims by some of the old timers that black bears were still around and I know from personal experience that we had at least one cougar who came and went at irregular intervals. One time it was chasing a big swamp rabbit up one of the mowed swaths between each row of trees while I was shearing with my long bladed knife. I stepped around a tree just as the cougar came charging up the path between the trees. I don't know which one of us was the most surprised or scared. All I know is that it went one way and I went the other and was glad of it. There were wolves, too, or what we called wolves. They were actually a mixture of red wolf, gray wolf, coyote and wild dog, a new species being formed. They loved new born calves, but that didn't bother us since I decided the first year I wasn't a real cowboy and sold the few cows we had bought.

Besides all those varmints and creatures we had ... coyotes. We could hear them howling every night. Sometimes we'd see them from a distance, but not often; they were wary. All except one. It was a huge coyote, the largest I've ever seen, even in zoos, and bigger than the ones the ranchers displayed when they managed to shoot one or two of a pack going after a newborn calf. It was a reddish gold color with the typical darker gray shading about the shoulders and flanks. Its legs were tawny and sturdy and its tail was a mixture of gold and gray. The animal's pelt was shiny and glowing with good health. I first saw it one day at lunch, strolling across our back yard as unconcerned as if it owned the place and paying no attention to the yipping of our little miniature dachshunds. It went on about its business while I thought to myself *what a beautiful animal*. It was that much of an eye-catcher.

I told Hannah about the big healthy coyote that evening after I came in from a bloody bout with the tractor, which I lost, as usual. Any time I got through the day without shedding blood from some piece of equipment, I counted it a success. She doctored my cuts and bruises and said she'd watch for the coyote.

The next day Hannah saw it. "You were right, Bob" she told me. "It really is a beautiful animal. It's almost like it was tame once, the way it goes ambling through our yard."

I suppose it was possible, but not likely. Coyotes may be seen in zoos or in some of those roadside exhibits along secondary highways that tourists like to stop at for no good reason I can think of, but they don't tame well. All you have to do is look at their eyes through the chain link fences to know that. "One of the ranchers'll shoot it if it has the same attitude on their place as it does on ours," I said.

"Oh, no! That would be a shame," Hannah said.

I agreed, but there was nothing to do about it. Besides, the coyote looked as if it could take care of itself well enough without our help. From then on we saw it from time to time, almost always coming from the hundred foot wide tree line between our house and the first Christmas tree field. I figured the coyote and its mate might have had a litter of pups. I didn't know right offhand whether coyotes were like wolves in that both male and female help in raising the pups, but thought it likely. I knew the coyote almost had to be a male as big as it was, almost the size of a wolf. And one day when it stopped to look curiously at our yapping little dachshunds, I got a good look at it and confirmed to myself it was a male.

For a few months we saw the coyote so regularly that it began to seem almost like an old friend, then one day it disappeared. I thought maybe one of the neighbors had shot it and for weeks I looked for hovering vultures. I even went to see what they had spotted on the couple of occasions when I saw them circling in the sky. In neither case was it the coyote, which made me glad. It was such a beautiful animal that it seemed like it should go on living forever. Several times it had stopped while crossing the yard long enough for me to get a real good look and I saw something else different about it. More different than it already was, I mean. Both ears had a sort of notch, as if someone had clipped out a piece of them. If it had been just one ear, I would have thought the notch was caused by an injury, but it was the same on both. Same size and with the same even margins. After the coyote had left and I thought about it some, I decided it must have been a birth defect of some kind, or maybe a harmless mutation. Whatever, it certainly didn't hurt its appearance; it only made it all the more striking.

Eventually, of course, we began to forget about the animal, only occasionally making a reference to it, wondering whether it had been killed or had just gone elsewhere to make a living. I didn't think so, though, since we still had plenty of rabbits. I saw them almost every day along the tree lines, coming out to feed in the mornings and evenings. Where you see rabbits, you'll find coyotes. Rabbits are their natural prey.

It was that fall before I saw another coyote, the one I don't like to think about. It was the day when the tractor took me for that unintended ride down to the bottom of the hill. It drove me along the edge of where the trees were planted, then turned left, to where one of the huge old oaks came into full view. The bottom part of the hill, beyond a mowed swath where the Christmas trees ended, was covered with brush and brambles and vines so thick a rabbit could hardly get through them. Just about that time the tractor slowed down, and came to a stop. I decided it was just being contrary, like tractors are with me. I reached for the throttle, thinking maybe I had bumped it but my hand never got that far.

Just at the edge of my peripheral vision I saw some movement. I looked around and my heart came to a full stop. I quit breathing and I damn near wet myself. It was a coyote, but like no coyote I had ever seen. I think it may have been old but there was no way of telling. It was in terrible condition. Its pelt was ragged, growing in muddy patches. It was blind in one eye, a dead white glaze covering the whole orb. The other eye was weeping a thick yellow ochre. Its tail hung low, as if it hadn't the strength to lift it up to its normal position. It took a limping step toward me, causing me to glance toward its feet. One of its front legs had been injured, or perhaps it was just a growth. Whatever, a big scabby mass covered the bottom of the leg where its toes and paw should have been.

As I sat there on the tractor, it took another step in my direction, not the least bit afraid. And it was only fifteen or twenty feet from me to begin with. Then it raised its head slowly and looked directly at me. I felt like I had suddenly fallen into a Stephen King novel. I wanted to get out of there. I didn't even have my pistol with me like I used to carry when I first started farming. I stared at the mangy coyote while my hand fumbled with the hand throttle and at the same time I pushed on the foot throttle with my boot toe. All that did was kill the motor. I grabbed for the key starter with my hands shaking so badly I could barely hold on to it. The tractor muttered and grumbled and stuttered and growled but finally came back to life. I put it in reverse and started to turn around, but took a final look at the coyote to be sure it wasn't going to attack me. And that's when I noticed the notched ears, just like the young, beautiful coyote we had seen so often earlier in the year.

It can't be the same one, I thought. *It couldn't have deteriorated that much in so short a time.* Nevertheless, the specter held my gaze as if it knew me from days gone by. I shivered, just wanting to get the hell out of there but then ... it began to change.

I sat on the tractor, mesmerized, as the ravaged coyote grew larger, then slowly raised its head ... and continued raising it. Its tail drooped lower and sank out of sight. Its front legs lifted from the ground, higher and higher. The coyote grew even more, becoming taller and standing on its hind legs. The mangy pelt changed into a ragged pair of pants and shirt. They were filthy with dirt and stains and hung on to what the coyote was changing into—an old, old man, with one arm held close to his chest. A fungus-like growth fused the fingers of that hand together. His hair was long and stringy, hanging in lank, dirty tangles from a partially bald head. His lips were cracked and a yellowish serum oozed from the cracks like unset glue. They parted, revealing rotten stumps of broken and decayed teeth. On his forehead I saw a ... I blinked, not wanting to believe it. It was a scar, the same scar I saw every morning in the mirror while shaving, a relic of the time I was working on the tractor's diesel engine and the hood had caught a gust of wind and come loose from its prop and fallen, gouging a big piece of skin and flesh from my forehead.

There was something else familiar about the apparition but I couldn't put my finger on it for a moment. Then it hit me. The rotten old man looked like my Dad as he was when he was found dead beneath a bridge in Houston, a homeless old drunk. The thing grinned around its worn stumps of teeth and uttered something unintelligible. Or maybe not. It sounded too much like it was saying *"You, Bob. I'm you."*

I think I screamed. I know I closed my eyes, wishing for nothing so much as my gun, or any kind of weapon to wipe that horror from the face of the earth. The only thing I had was a lit cigarette. I threw it. Surprisingly, it went where I intended it to, right in the face of that scary old son of a bitch. The red hot tip hit him just below the left eye. He raised his hand to knock it away but was slow. What happened was that his hand slapped the lit cigarette hard against his cheek, pushing it into the skin and leaving the red coal behind, stuck to his face, while the rest of it crumbled and fell off. The sickly stench of burning flesh filled the air.

At the same time, I felt a horrible burning pain on my cheek. I thought a wasp must have stung me while my eyes were closed. I certainly didn't connect the pain to the cigarette I threw at the hideous old man. The pain got me moving and for once the tractor did what it was supposed to. It chugged back up the hill and headed for home while I held my hand to my face and wished I hadn't drank the last of my water a few minutes ago so I could put something cool on that throbbing spot on my cheek.

When I got to the house the first thing I did was go to the bathroom and look at my face. There was a burned spot just beneath my left eye. A big blister was forming. Cigarette ashes were embedded in it.

While I was standing there wondering how it had happened, Hannah came in and saw me.

"What happened?" she asked.

"I don't know," I confessed. "There was … never mind. It's just that all of a sudden I felt a really bad pain below my eye and came on back. See?" I turned so she could get a look at it.

Hannah peered at the mark. "It looks like a cigarette burn. Have you started smoking again?"

Then I remembered throwing that lit cigarette at the old man. I felt in my pockets. There were no cigarettes there. I had quit smoking years ago. "No. I haven't been smoking. I don't know what happened."

But I did, of course, even if I couldn't explain it. A young, handsome coyote that disappears. An old, horribly aged coyote that transforms itself into an aged, liquor-ravaged wreck of a man that resembled my Dad, and perhaps was what I'd look like in thirty or forty years. But there was only a six month gap between when the young coyote quit coming around and when I saw its old self, with the same notched ears, which then turned into a relic of my dead father. And the burn I gave the old man from my tossed cigarette that I don't know how I happened to have. I had quit smoking years ago, at the same time I gave up liquor. Then the cigarette burn on my own face, with the ashes still embedded in it.

Six months? Is there anything that could possibly turn me into that kind of wreck in only six months? Surely not. I thought I must have had a waking dream. But if that was so, how to explain the burn?

Hannah must have seen the panic in my eyes. She hugged me and I held her close, trying to make the memories go away. It didn't help. I'm still scared. Scared almost to death. So scared that I've started drinking heavily again. And yesterday I bought a pack of cigarettes. When the coyotes start their howling at night I wake in a blind panic and reach for my bottle and smokes. One night, after Hannah finally left me, I passed out with my arm hanging over the edge of the bed and dropped a lit cigarette into the waste basket. I woke up only after my hand was burned so horribly that the fingers fused together with scar tissue. After it healed, it looked like ... I didn't want to think about what it looked like. Nor what the rest of me was beginning to look like, either. In a drunken rage, I went through the house and broke every mirror I could find, crying and cursing all the while.

Now I spend most of my time sitting on the porch, smoking and drinking, with a rifle across my knees, waiting. On what, I don't know. But if I see a coyote, I'll shoot it.

The End

Both those coyotes were real. Curiously, after writing this story neither of them ever made another appearance.

My printer wouldn't work one morning. I spent an hour with the damned thing, punching buttons, opening windows and following arcane directions, trying this and that and it just sat there and sulled like an old possum. Finally I got disgusted and said "Okay, you stupid printer, I'll fix you. I'll just cut off your juice for a while and see how you like it." So I did. I unplugged it and let it sit until I felt like fooling with it again. I plugged it back in and it worked perfectly. Just another gremlin, I thought. Gremlin? Hmm. Could I make a story out of a gremlin? About that time Betty came into the office and kissed me. Mmm, I thought. Cupid's busy already this morning. Cupid? Could I make a story out of Cupid? I thought for a while and finally wrote one of the very few fantasies of my career.

OOPS!

"Sonofabitch! Goddamned thing won't boot up again."

"Hit it. That's what you always do."

Jerry Wilson glared at his co-worker and pounded the CPU with his fist. It promptly booted up.

Beatrice Tomlin snickered. "See?"

"Yeah. But why sometimes and not others? The damned thing is driving me crazy."

"There's a gremlin in it." She said and laughed. She stood up and pushed her office chair back. "I'm going home for lunch. Want me to bring you anything?"

He glanced at his watch. "Go ahead. I'm not hungry now."

"Maybe you'd like me to make you dinner tonight?"

"Thanks but I've already made plans."

"Okay. Be back in a bit."

Jerry and Beatrice were the sole employees and also the co-owners of the little computer shop in the small town of Borderlon, Texas. Contrary to gossip, there was nothing romantic about the relationship even though Beatrice had thoughts in that direction. Jerry wouldn't play, though. He knew she was looking for a husband and children and he wanted nothing of the sort regardless of how attractive she was. He resisted her moves on him with great dexterity (and some reluctance, given her 100111-10111-100101 measurements) while continuing to play the field.

The door closed behind her and he turned back to the problem he thought he'd fixed twice already, the computer that was reluctant to boot up on demand. It seemed that a good cursing and pounding on the CPU was the only solution but he could hardly tell the customer that. He had taken the damned thing apart twice and found nothing wrong, then sent it home with its owner only to have him back in the next day growling that it wasn't fixed. Mr. Clemmons was becoming very aggravated with him. In fact, he suggested that if it weren't properly repaired this time he just might find another place to have it worked on.

"Like he could find another shop in this burg," Jerry muttered to himself. "Still, he could give us some bad publicity. Goddamned Gremlin, that's what it is. If I could talk to the little bastard I'd give it what for, all right. Screwing up my work and making me look like a dork."

A little blue cloud materialized over the recalcitrant computer. Jerry's eyes bugged out as it took shape. It grew hands and feet and a head with merry eyes and pointed ears. It was dressed in a long sleeved blue tunic and bloused trousers of a lighter blue. Ankle-high gray shoes with curled up tips and a rakish little pointy hat with a narrow brim completed its dress. Its skin was pink, its long-fingered hands were a darker pink. It had a face with a bulbous little red nose and eyes of bright, bright green set below tangled black eyebrows the same color as its hair.

"Close your mouth before you swallow a fly, Bud." The specter said. It settled down on top of the CPU and crossed its short pudgy legs.

"Gug," Jerry said.

"Gug? Hell, I thought you wanted to talk to me. I don't know what *gug* means."

"What ... who ... where ... how...?" Jerry uttered.

"That's not a hell of a lot better, Didn't you want to give me what for?"

"I ... a Gremlin? You're a *Gremlin*?"

"In the flesh. Er, sort of."

"A real Gremlin!"

"Look, Bud, I don't got all day. You want to cuss me, get on with it. I got other stuff to screw up, you know."

Jerry squinted one eye, then the other. He didn't know if there was really such a thing as a gremlin but if not, this apparition would do until a real one came along. He gathered his courage.

"How come Gremlins always want to fuck with things?"

"What things?"

"This damn computer, that's what!" Jerry said, pointing at the guilty CPU the gremlin was sitting on. "Are you the one causing it to boot up only when it takes a notion?"

"Yep, that's me. I done it."

"But ... but why?"

It shrugged. "I like to fuck with things. That's what Gremlins do."

"Well, how about stopping it? I've got a business to run."

The Gremlin rubbed its pointy chin and wriggled its bulbous nose as if considering a grave question. "What'll you give me if I stop?"

"Huh?"

"I don't like repeating myself, Bud. You heard me."

"What'll I give you?"

A look of long suffering exasperation appeared on its face. It motioned with a hand toward its chest. "Right. What'll you give me?"

"Well, uh. Uh. Well, what do you want?"

"Nothing."

"But you asked..."

"Doesn't mean I want anything you can give. Tell you what, though. Suppose I be nice and leave this piece of junk alone. How does that sound?"

Jerry looked at it suspiciously. "And then what?"

"That's my business," it smirked. "Just remember, Yin and Yang. Plus and Minus. Everything has a consequence."

"And this is my business." He thought of how irate Mr. Clemmons would be if he returned and his computer still wasn't fixed. Besides, the Gremlin couldn't cause much more trouble than it already had. "Alright, already. Leave it alone. Okay?"

"Glad to be of help. It's done." There was a pop of displaced air and the gremlin disappeared.

Jerry slowly eased his body into his chair. He stared at the CPU. It sat innocently on the work table. He punched the on button. It booted up.

Beatrice sighed as she sat down at her kitchen table with a sandwich and glass of tea. It was so frustrating being hung up on a guy who was avoiding commitment like the proverbial plague, going so far as not allowing himself to even have dinner with her for fear of finding himself in front of a preacher before it was over. Damn his big brown bedroom eyes," she muttered between bites, "not to mention his broad shoulders, slim waist and tight buns. And oh yes, his handsome face and keen intelligence. Have I mentioned that?"

"Nope, not on my watch, but now that you have, I can only agree."

"Eeek! Who's here?" She rose half way from the table, almost tipping over her tea. She looked frantically around the room.

The voice spoke again, this time seeming to be muttering to itself. "Damned uppity little good looking bastard, making himself visible and playing hard to get. Nothing I can't do, too."

"Who is it? Who said that?" Beatrice turned in a circle gazing frantically for the source of the voice.

"I said it, Cutie. Hey! Up here!"

Beatrice trained her gaze toward the ceiling. There, hanging in space above the table on tiny, lightly fluttering white wings was a Cupid, straight from the pages of innumerable stories and cartoons. The only difference was that this Cupid (Cupette?) was female rather than male. She was about a half meter in height and possessed a nice but slightly chubby body. It was completely unadorned. Well, she did have a quiver full of arrows slung over one nicely rounded little shoulder but that was all. Her face was heart-shaped with red lips and nicely flushed cheeks. She was as pretty as a miniature, slightly overweight September Morn of photographer's fame but her hair was taffy-blond and shoulder-length. It waved gently in the breeze from the movement of the diminutive wings that didn't look large enough to keep a hummingbird aloft, much less a Cupid.

"I don't believe it! I don't, I don't!"

"You don't? Then I guess you don't need my help with that hunk you've been mooning over so long, huh?"

"I … I…" Beatrice's mind raced. *Help? With a hunk? Did she mean…?* "Are you talking about Jerry?"

"You mooning over anyone else, Cutie?"

"No! I mean … I must be going crazy. You look like Cupid."

"No reason I shouldn't. I *am* Cupid."

"I thought Cupid was a male."

"Nope, the artists all got it wrong. See?"

"No, I don't see! You can't be real!"

"Want to pinch me?"

"No!"

"Want Jerry to pinch you?"

"No! I mean yes! I mean … what do you want, anyway?" She sat back down, fearing she would fall down if she didn't.

"It's not what I want, Cutie. It's you that's doing the mooning." The self-professed Cupid crossed her legs in mid-air. "Hmmm? Isn't that right?"

"For all the good it does me, yes, damn it."

"So, want some help, huh?"

"I wish."

"That's what I thought. Okay, I'll take care of it."

"Wait! What are you going to do?"

Cupid (or Cupette) assumed an air of long-suffering patience. "What do you think I'm going to do? I don't carry this bow in my hand and that quiver of arrows over my shoulder for nothing. Damned thing, strap always getting in the way of my boobs. Sometimes I wonder why I do it."

"Why do you?"

"Why do I do what? Shoot arrows at idiots to make them realize they're in love?"

"Well, yes."

It shrugged. "That's what Cupids do."

Beatrice closed her eyes then covered her face with her hands for good measure.

"What's wrong, Cutie? Afraid to ask?"

"Yes! I mean, no!"

"You want me to take a shot at the hunk, huh?"

She nodded helplessly. "At Jerry."

"Who did you think I meant? The meter reader?"

"No. At Jerry! God, this is crazy!"

"That's love, Cutie. Crazy as all get-out. Shall we get on with it? I've got other people to see. I can't sit here jibber-jabbering all day. There are other love-sick idiots I've gotta take care of."

"What will the hunk, um, er, I mean what will Jerry think when he sees you?"

"Get real. Who ever admits to seeing Cupid? Anyhow, you'd be surprised what he's been seeing. Everything except the love of his life. If you're finished with that sandwich, let's go, Cutie."

She got up from the table and pulled on her jacket. Still bemused, she left her apartment and began walking the three short blocks back to the shop.

Jerry looked up from where she had left him when she went to lunch. He was still turning the CPU on and off.

"Is it fixed?" Beatrice asked, more for something to say than anything else. It worked perfectly every time he touched the start/stop button.

"Yup. It's fixed."

"What was wrong with it?"

"A Gremlin."

"Right." She rolled her eyes then hastily averted them as she saw Cupid overhead, fumbling an arrow out of her quiver. She gulped, settled down at her desk and began fooling with a software program. Men! He took no notice of how agitated she was or how she kept glancing up into the air to see how Cupid was doing. Or not doing. She seemed to be having trouble getting an arrow loose.

"Ouch! Damned things. Always poking me in the boobs," she mumbled and began fitting the arrow she had finally gotten loose onto the string of the tiny bow. It didn't look big enough or powerful enough to shoot a missile two feet, but then it would be shooting down, not up. That ought to do it, she thought. Maybe. I hope.

Jerry took no notice of Cupid's comment but he did peer inquisitively at Beatrice as if finally noticing her agitation. She looked hurriedly away then back again. Now he seemed to be staring at the top of the CPU that had been giving him so much trouble. He said something she didn't quite understand.

"Ah, now if he'll just hold still..." Cupid said in a barely audible voice.

"Ouch!" the Gremlin said.

"Uh oh," Cupid said. "Sorry. I never was much of a shot."

Beatrice stared in utter amazement at the tiny little being who had suddenly materialized atop the CPU. The arrow from Cupid's bow was stuck firmly in the tiny, oddly dressed little man's chest. He stared down at the arrow in horror.

"I didn't meant to!" Cupid said loudly. "I was aiming for the hunk! Hey! Why are you looking at me like that?!"

"What's that thing sticking out of your chest?" Jerry said to the Gremlin. His look of befuddlement was genuine. It went perfectly with Beatrice's countenance. She was radiating disgust. Three feet away and she missed! And hit whatever that thing was.

"You missed, damn it!" Beatrice shouted, uncaring of what Jerry might think. The situation had rapidly gone to hell. "Shoot again!"

"Who is that wiggly little thing in the air with the thick waist and that toy bow and arrow?" Jerry said to the Gremlin.

"Thick waist? She's got a perfect waist, you Dummy!"

"Who is that?" Beatrice asked. "How did it get in here?"

"I might ask you the same thing," Jerry said, pointing at the Cupid. "And she does too have a thick waist. And her boobs are too small." He raised his brows at Beatrice.

"That's it, brother," Cupid said. "Small boobs, huh? Now it's your turn." She let fly with another arrow. It hit Jerry squarely over the heart.

"Ouch!" he said.

"Serves you right, Bud," the Gremlin said. "Hey Cupid, let's blow this burg and go pitch some woo."

"Sounds like a good idea to me, Sweetie," Jerry said to Beatrice. "Let's close up shop and go breathe heavy." He had completely forgotten about the gremlin and the other little being.

"Not without a preacher," Cupid said to the Gremlin.

"Not without a preacher," Beatrice said smugly to Jerry. *Hooked, by God!*

"Alright, already, we'll see a preacher," the Gremlin said to the Cupette. "Let's go!"

The two small beings disappeared in puffs of pink and blue smoke.

Beatrice hooked her arm with Jerry's. "Let's go, Big Boy."

And they all lived happily ever afterward.

Without a single Gremlin ever bothering Jerry and Beatrice again.

The End

Someone who really likes to write fantasy could probably make a novel of something like this and do a better job. Betty said she thought it was cute, but then what else is a woman going to say about Cupid except maybe sweet?

If you don't like stories with a unhappy ending you may skip this one. I just wrote it when I was thinking of how humans would react upon seeing a real alien. Probably not very nice considering the way we treat each other on this old globe.

RETRIBUTION

There was a scream, loud and intrusive, waking him from his Saturday morning nap. At first he thought it was a dream but then he heard it again and knew it was his wife's voice.

"Jim! Jim, come quick! Hurry! Eeeek! Get away from me!"

James Trevers bounced from the bed, still befogged by sleep but rapidly coming to his senses. *Burglar*, he thought. *Ellen! Little Randy*! He ran to his closet and reached high up to the back of the top shelf. He felt around in panic then breathed a sigh of relief when his hand closed on the grip of the little automatic. He grabbed it and began running toward Ellen's bathroom where the screams had come from.

"Get away! Get away!" Ellen cried. "Jiiiiimmm!"

He burst through the door to her bathroom, expecting to see a rapist ripping at Ellen's nightgown, bloody knife at her throat.

The swinging door hit his wife squarely in the ass, knocking her forward. Her shins hit the commode and she fell over it, smacking her head on the sheet rock wall on the other side.

James waved the pistol in a circle, looking for the miscreant, ready to kill. Ellen moaned and tried to sit up. She blinked her eyes and saw her husband. "Jim! Get it! Kill it! Hit it!"

"What is it? Has he gone?"

"No, no! There it is! Kill it!"

His gaze followed Ellen's pointing finger and landed on the shelf adjacent to the wash basin. There, sitting with apparent unconcern was the subject of his wife's hysteria. At least he thought it was sitting. It could have been squatting, or possibly lying down for all he knew. It had an indeterminate number of appendages that moved slowly this way and that. Two, or possibly three short wiggly antennae sprouted from a lump that appeared to emerge from a body in no particular order, for it was moving, too. The lump sported four bulges that may have been eyes but could just as well have been bug bites. It was spotted with little red and green ovals in a pattern, he thought, but the more he stared the less they made sense.

"Aren't you going to kill it?" With her husband present and holding a weapon, Ellen didn't have quite such a sense of overwhelming terror. In fact, the ... the ... whatever it was seemed almost friendly if it was looked at in a certain way.

"You really want me to kill it?" Jim asked. It didn't seem particularly threatening.

"Wait. I was just scared. Maybe it won't hurt us. But what is it?"

"It's a little monster is what it is," Jim said, changing his mind. "I'd better shoot it."

"No, don't. It may be friendly." She reached out her hand and very gingerly touched the creature on a part of its body that she first made certain was toothless.

"Queep?" The critter said.

"*Queep?* What does that mean?" Ellen said.

"Queep. Queep. Queep?"

"Bullshit," Jim said. "Queep to you, too."

"Don't talk so mean to it, dear. What if it's someone's pet that got lost?"

"That thing is no pet. Besides, how'd it get in here?"

Goofy, the miniature dachshund who shared their home entered the fray, if fray it was. "Woof!" he barked.

"Queep!" the critter answered while moving about on the shelf.

"Woof! Woof!" Goofy barked some more, but it was a friendly bark, the one he used to greet Lambkins, Ellen's neutered cat.

"Queep!" The creature moved all its appendages at once and suddenly flew off the shelf and through the air, landing squarely on Goofy's back.

"Woof!" Goofy barked and began running through the house like an extremely small horse with a miniature rodeo clown attached.

"Goofy! Come back here!" Jim yelled. He got no better results than he ever did when he commanded the short haired dachshund to do something.

"Woof! Woof!" Goofy barked as he came tearing back up the hall chasing Lambkins, who now had the rider.

"Meow! Meow!" Lambkins said, which is cat talk for "That short legged little pest couldn't catch me if I were walking, even with a thing on my back!"

Lambkins stopped and began rubbing against Jim's leg with the odd looking monster still sitting on it. But not for long.

The queep-emitting critter jumped off Lambkins and quickly fixed a number of appendages on Ellen's leg and began crawling up it. To her it felt like a big spider. Ellen hated spiders.

"Jim! Kill it! Kill it! It's like a spider! It's crawling all over me!" She hit at the wiggling little being and knocked it loose.

"Queep!" it uttered loudly and jumped back onto her leg. Ellen screamed again.

Jim stepped closer and pointed his pistol at it, making certain his wife wasn't in the line of fire. The sound of the .22 caliber shot resembled a twelve gauge shotgun in the narrow confines of the bathroom.

The creature dropped from Ellen's leg and crumpled to the floor, coiling up in a ball. It shuddered all over. A trickle of orange fluid spilled from its body and then it was still.

Goofy nosed the carcass and whined.

Lambkins patted the body with a forepaw and meowed.

Ellen stared at the thing. She remembered hollering at her husband the second time, admonishing him to kill the creature when it felt like a big spider on her leg. She also remembered that it hadn't really hurt her. Not at all.

"Jim! Why did you shoot the poor thing? I was just excited. I didn't mean it."

"You said to shoot it, for Chrissake! You said it felt like you had a spider on you. I know how you hate spiders."

Ellen looked on the remains. Now she felt sad and her expression showed it. She wondered how it would have fitted into the household if it had been allowed to live. The pets had seemed to enjoy it.

Jim began feeling guilty. "I'll go bury it," he said. He went back to the bedroom, thankful that their three year-old son had slept through the racket. He put up his pistol and pulled on a pair of pants. He found a plastic bag and deposited the remains in it. He rooted around in the garage until he remembered he had left the spade out by the flower bed. He found it and dug a hole. Just as he lifted the bag with the body to deposit it in the shallow grave he heard a noise behind him. He turned around.

A larger version of the little creature stood, or perhaps squatted, or maybe lay near him. Its appendages all wiggled vigorously. "Quaap!" it said. "Quaap! Quaap! Quaap!"

"Bullshit. Quaap to you, too. Go away. Go back to wherever you came from. You things scared my wife half to death," Jim said, but he was remembering how Ellen had touched the other odd little creature and how it had rode on Goofy and Lambkins, apparently having a good time.

"Quaap!" The larger replica of whatever it was he had shot turned and ran, or waddled or perhaps scuttled toward the back door.

"Hey! Come back here!" Jim yelled, chasing after it.

The creature was surprisingly speedy and it seemed to know exactly where it was going. It passed through the door as if it were made of air while Jim had to stop and open it. He stumbled up the stairs in pursuit.

Little Randy's room! That's where it's going, he thought. I guess it wants to play, too. He hurried after it, thinking it might accidentally hurt Randy like Goofy occasionally did when he and their son got to scuffling too vigorously, or like Lambkins had scratched him once when he tugged too vigorously on her tail.

Sure enough, it oozed through little Randy's bedroom door without slowing down. Jim ran after it and opened it. He flicked on the light. Randy was in his small bed, still fast asleep.

The creature hopped up onto the bed with his son. It pulled a little device from somewhere within the folds of its body. Before Jim could make a single move, it pointed the gadget toward Randy. There was a buzzing sound and a streak of blue light sang a song of death, punching a hole through little Randy's heart, killing him instantly.

Jim cried out. Ellen screamed as she came into the room and saw what had happened. Goofy whimpered. Lambkins scurried under Randy's bed and yowled.

"Why? Why did it do that?" Jim sobbed. "Why did it kill our son?" He looked around but the creature was already gone. His gaze crossed to the window. Through it he saw something like a large blue egg the size of a lawn tractor rise into the sky and fade from sight.

Ellen's mouth dropped open as she saw the egg vanish. *Son. Killed.* The odd little creature that looked exactly like the bigger one except for size. Revelation came to her in a burst of horror and remorse.

"You killed its son," she said through her sobs as she clung to her husband. "I told you to kill its son and you did and now it's killed Randy. It killed our son in retribution." She began crying, thinking of how she had screamed for Jim to murder the little creature that hadn't really hurt her. It had only wanted to play.

Jim looked at the body of his son. He thought of his gun in the closet. Gently, he disentangled Ellen from her grasp on him and headed toward their bedroom. Ellen watched him go, knowing what he was after, what he intended. She made no attempt to stop him. She waited quietly, crying, for him to come back with his gun.

The End

Well, you can't say I didn't warn you...

It is very rare for me to write a fiction story based on a real happening around the farm. In this case, Robyn is our grandchild and she did find a "special" rock on the road one day and Betty and I have kept it on a shelf for over twenty years. The rest of the story is fiction—I hope!

ROBYN'S ROCK

Retirement is good in a number of ways. You can get up when you want to or go to bed when you want to and there's no particular routine you have to follow if doesn't suit your fancy. Still, it has drawbacks. If you're not normally gregarious and don't attend church and also live in a rural area, then almost inevitably you're going to find yourself becoming more and more isolated, like we are here in East Texas. With our daughter Jennie working overseas and her own adult children, Robyn and Gretchen living in different states, Amanda and I both began to feel the loneliness creeping in. That's why company was always a welcome event for us, especially when the granddaughters visited. We loved to talk to them and listen to their dreams and aspirations. Their lives stretched endlessly before them, or so they thought. They had no conception of how fast the years would pass, or how soon they would be old folks just like us who wanted, even needed, company to brighten our routine and introduce a few changes into the same old routine.

The thing is, when we did have visitors, we almost always received a call in advance from whomever it was, telling us when they would arrive, how long they'd stay and so on. So it was a real surprise when the doorbell rang one day and our granddaughter Robyn stood there in the entrance, holding the handle of a suitcase that trailed behind her like a faithful little puppy. She was trying to smile at us but it wasn't going well. It looked forced, as if she was maybe hiding something. It didn't matter. We were glad to see her under any circumstances.

"Robyn!" Amada said, giving her a huge hug. "What a nice surprise! Come on in."

"Hi Grannie, hi Grandpa. I'm sorry I didn't call. I was in a hurry, sort of."

"It's okay, sweetheart," I said, giving her a hug in turn and taking her suitcase. I wheeled it on into the spare bedroom while Amanda busied herself in the kitchen, getting a fresh pot of coffee going, taking cookies from the freezer and popping them into the microwave and setting out cups and saucers. She didn't offer Robyn a soda. Unlike most kids of her generation, she preferred her caffeine in coffee, probably from her girlish imitation of us when she was younger.

When I returned, Robyn was still standing in the living room, a kind of blank expression on her face, as if just realizing she was here, but having no earthly idea why she'd come.

"Sit down, baby. You look tired," I said. I put my arm around her shoulder and led her over to the big couch, the one she always liked to curl up on and read when she was a child and we had her for a few days.

"I'm not really tired, Grandpa. In fact, I'm not really sure why I'm here, without even calling or anything. I just..." A puzzled expression crossed her face, like someone waking from a vivid dream and realizing they're back in the real world.

"Maybe you needed a rest, child," Amanda said. "You're looking a little peaked."

Robyn nodded, embarrassed. "I know, Grannie. I haven't slept much the last couple of days. I kept waking up and thinking I needed to come see you and Grandpa."

I smiled. "Well, you're here now. Feel any better?"

"I guess," she said miserably. "It's just so crazy. Danny said I was acting silly."

"Danny. Is that your new fellow?"

"Uh-huh. I've been seeing him a couple of months. Living with him, really. I wanted him to come with me, but he wouldn't. He said I was acting like a hysterical woman."

I could see tears beginning to gather in her eyelashes, ready to overflow.

Robyn is a pretty girl, tall and slim with honey-colored hair. I thought back to my youth and couldn't imagine any young man not wanting to accompany her, or do whatever it took to make her happy.

"Justin, honey, would you pour the coffee for us?" Amanda asked.

"Huh? Oh, sure." I got the hint. Mandy wanted to say a few words in private to Robyn. Of course she'd tell me later but she was thoughtful that way, not wanting to embarrass the girl if it was heart trouble of some sort, the emotional kind.

I busied myself longer than I really needed to, emptying the grounds and washing the basket, then pouring the coffee. After that I got down a thermal carafe to keep it fresh in case anyone wanted more. Personally, I thought Robyn could use a drink more than anything else. I was tempted to add a dollop of brandy her cup but resisted the impulse.

When I returned with the tray, Robyn was dry-eyed and it was my wife looking puzzled. It wasn't love problems, then. I set the tray down and passed out the cups and saucers of coffee.

Robyn hadn't taken more than a few sips when she stood up. She looked around the room, but her gaze stopped at the shelves on both sides of the big fireplace. They were cluttered with little knick knacks and keepsakes accumulated over the years. The shelves ran on around the room but the rest of them were occupied by books. She paid no attention to them, though ordinarily she made a bee-line to the books when she visited, wanting to see what was new since the last time.

"What is it, baby?" I asked. I was becoming concerned now. Something was clearly wrong. I hated to see it. I know grandparents aren't supposed to play favorites, but it had been hard to resist with Robyn. She loved to have us read to her as a little girl and the high point of any trip her parents made to see us was when we took her to our little local library. Gretchen, on the other hand, always preferred television.

"I don't *know*, Grandpa," she cried. "There's something..." She took a few hesitant steps toward the fireplace shelves, then turned to the one on the right. She stepped closer. I had stood up shortly after she did and was in a position that let me see the surprise lighting up her eyes. Her lips parted as if she wanted to say something but was having trouble getting the words out. She pointed toward one of the shelves.

"What's this, grandpa?"

I came over so I could see what was interesting her. I grinned. "Don't you remember that rock, Robyn? It's yours."

She shook her head. "No, but ... this is silly, Grandpa, but I think that's what I came here for, even if I don't remember it." She took a couple more baby steps until she was near enough to touch the rock but she hesitated. She looked at me, silently appealing for an explanation.

I thought back. "I guess you were about six at the time, Robyn. Your Mom and Dad came for a visit just after we had done some repair work on our road. We used a whole truckload of gravel, most of it about the same size as that rock there. It was a pretty day and your Grannie and I decided to walk up to the mailbox. You wanted to come along, so naturally we let you. As we were walking, you stopped suddenly and bent over. You picked up that rock and showed it to us. It was kind of an unusual shape and color, so it was easy to see why you spotted it. Anyway, you put it in the pocket of your jeans and when we got back to the house, you asked us if we'd keep it for you." I smiled fondly at her and to myself at the memory. "So I took your rock and put it on the shelf there. Ever since then Grannie and I have called it 'Robyn's Rock', and we made sure it never got thrown away. It's been on the shelf all these years." Robyn had just celebrated her 25th birthday.

Right then was the beginning of all the events surrounding and related to that rock. Robyn's Rock.

She reached out and plucked it from the shelf. She held it in her hand, examining it as if seeing it for the first time. For her, it probably seemed like the first look at it, for she had obviously forgotten all about asking us to keep it for her. Apparently the rock hadn't forgotten her, though. It was striated with different colored material in a dark brown base, about an inch long and a half inch in its other dimensions, like an irregular rectangular block. Granite, I thought, except I had a vague impression that granite was all one color. It was perfectly smooth, too, like many of the stones in gravel that size are, a result of being polished against other stones and running water from ancient streams.

"Oh!" Robyn exclaimed. "Oh, no!" She put the rock back in its place and turned to us for comfort. She was clearly frightened by something she had suddenly thought of, or perhaps was visualizing for the first time.

We gathered her into our arms and made soothing noises until she had settled down and was ready to talk. I led her over to the couch. Amanda and I sat on each side of her and each of us held one of her hands while she explained what had happened.

"As soon as I picked up the rock, I had a ... a vision, I guess you could call it. It's so real, though!"

"What was it, baby?" Amanda asked, concern tingeing her every word.

"Oh, it can't be, but it seems so true! There's going to be an earthquake in California day after tomorrow, right near Los Angeles where Danny and I live. That's what I saw in my mind when I picked up the rock. I'm *still* seeing it! It's like I *know* it's going to happen. And it's going to be awful!"

I let go of her hand long enough to tamp tobacco into my pipe and get it going. Robyn smiled tentatively at me and I knew she was remembering all the times she told me how good the smoke from my pipe smelled.

But Amanda wasn't smiling. "What do you think, Justin?"

What was I supposed to say? I've been around long enough to know there's lots of things that can't be explained through our normal senses. Things we write off as "coincidence" most of the time unless there's a belief in the supernatural and psychic ability or such. I wasn't the kind of person who held with mediums or little men with big eyes being held captive in area 51, that sort of stuff. On the other hand I was damn certain I didn't know everything in the world, either. Besides, Robyn was a level-headed girl and always had been. She'd rather die than have anyone think she went along with such nonsense. Yet here she was, experiencing just such an occurrence herself, and telling us in no uncertain terms what was going to happen. It certainly gave me pause to think.

"Justin, Robyn wouldn't say something like this for a joke or come all the way out here from California on a whim. Don't you think we should warn folks about this?"

"Mandy, sweetie, who do you think would believe us? We know Robyn, but what would you think if someone you didn't know started predicting earthquakes? What if some stranger tried to warn us to leave home because they thought an earthquake was coming? Would you listen to them?"

Amanda's shoulders slumped. While she might take stuff like this more seriously than I ever would, she's still a sensible woman. She knew as well as I did what kind of reaction we'd get if we started shouting "Earthquake!" to the California authorities, especially from Texas!

Robyn began crying, the hopeless sort of sobbing a person does in a situation there's no help for. I put my arm around her and held her to my chest while she let the grief inside her pour out in tears.

Amanda handed her some tissues to wipe her eyes and blow her nose when she recovered from the heartache of knowing something terrible was going to happen, but realizing just as we did that no one would believe her.

"Justin, I think we should try warning people out there. It's the least we can do. I don't mind being taken for a fool if it doesn't happen, but if it does, I couldn't live with myself if I hadn't at least tried."

I looked our granddaughter in the eye, trying to gauge the seriousness of her belief. Thoughts of schizophrenia briefly crossed my mind before I discarded them. She had never shown the slightest tendency toward mental illness of any kind. "You really believe this?"

"Grandpa, it isn't like believing. I *know* it's going to happen, no matter how crazy it sounds." She trembled, as if seeing it in her mind, the tumbled homes, fallen overpasses, the panic and loss of life a major earthquake would cause.

She had told us it would be awful. "You said it's going to be awful. Is that what you really think? Be sure, now."

She nodded, misery written on her face like that you see in the news sometimes of young people who have just suffered a major catastrophe for the first time in their lives. Misery coupled with disbelief that such a thing could ever happen to them. I drew on my pipe and blew smoke into the air. I watched it coil and separate into wreaths and eddies from the slow movement of air in the room. I shrugged. "Well, if Mandy says we should try warning folks, I guess we better. I'm like her—I'd never forgive myself if we didn't try and it really does happen."

Robyn hugged each of us. Tears glittered in her eyes again, but this time they were those of relief that we believed her. Or at least were willing to go out on a limb to support her vision.

It didn't do any good, of course. Every newspaper and radio station and political figure we managed to contact listened for a moment, then thanked us politely and hung up. Many didn't even wait until we'd finished, not even when we told them the exact time the earthquake would happen. Robyn said she knew. Day after tomorrow, Friday, four thirteen in the afternoon, their time, six thirteen for us. Despairing, we began calling friends and relatives in California, those living anywhere near Los Angeles. There were quite a few. Amanda's sister, one of her nieces, several of my old army buddies I'd kept in touch with. Some internet friends. A few others Amanda and I had met over the course of our lives. Robyn called her circle of friends and her boyfriend Danny, of course. He laughed it off, just like the rest of them did.

All the next day and the following morning, Robyn urged us to keep trying. We did, to the honest limits of our ability and she helped all she could. We may as well not have said a word for all the good it did us. By Friday afternoon we were all mental wrecks. As the hands on the clock approached six o'clock I brought a fresh carafe of coffee into the living room. This time I used big mugs and I did add brandy to the coffee, a jigger in each big mug. We turned on the television at six and waited. The tension built up like the last few seconds of a tied game in the Superbowl, where your favorite team is lining up to try blocking a long field goal that would win the game for their opponent.

We were tuned to CNN news where I thought we'd get the first notice of the earthquake when and if it happened. By then I believed almost as staunchly as Robyn, and so did Amada. I felt a chill moving through my body and shivered. I took another big gulp of my coffee, glad now that I'd added the brandy. It warmed my insides and the shivering stopped.

Six thirteen. The news reader continued as before. Six fourteen. Six fifteen. Nothing, but Robyn was huddled against Mandy, her head turned away from the television. She said she couldn't bear to watch. Six sixteen, and I began to relax. It seemed she had been wrong after all.

The reader suddenly stopped in the middle of a story about the Middle East that none of us were paying attention to. She cocked her head to the side as if listening to someone out of camera range, but it was most likely a feed through the unobtrusive earpiece she wore. She turned back to face her unseen audience.

> *"We have a special announcement of breaking news. All communication with an area of California centered near the city of Los Angeles and Palmdale has been disrupted. We have reports from affiliates further north that an earthquake has occurred. We do not yet know the epicenter, nor the severity, but from the lack of news coming from the region, we suspect it happened near Los Angeles."*

An aide appeared on camera and slipped her a sheet of yellow foolscap. She glanced at it for a moment then looked back up.

> *"We have received a number of cell phone reports from residents in the Los Angeles area. According*

*to them there has been an earthquake of major
proportions. One caller tells of a number of office
buildings that have fallen. Others are reporting
from collapsed apartment houses, begging for help
for people trapped in the ruins. Attempts to reach
authorities in Las Angeles have been fruitless so
far. From numerous reports we are assuming
many public buildings in the city are in ruins, with
perhaps the mayor and other functionaries still at
work when the earthquake occurred."*

Robyn was holding her face in her hands, crying her heart
out. Mandy and I looked at each other across her shoulders,
helpless, still not quite believing it had actually happened, just
at the time and place Robyn had predicted. I thought of
Mandy's sister and apparently she did too, almost at the same
moment. She began trying to reach her on her cell phone
number but it was hopeless. Probably millions of people
across the country were also trying to call.

"You told them. You told them and told them," Robyn
sobbed. "I told Danny and he just laughed at me, damn him!"

"Everyone laughed at us, too, baby. We did everything we
possibly could. That's all anyone can do, so let it go. Try not to
blame them or blame yourself."

She nodded, understanding but still upset. She was mad
and frightened and grieving for all the friends and
acquaintances who might have been hurt. I could understand.
There's nothing like not knowing to compound a tragedy.

We stuck by the television well into the night. More and
more information from the area filtered into the major news
nodes, coming from cell phones, the internet and news teams
sent in with their equipment. It had indeed been a major

quake. Many areas of Los Angeles appeared to be in ruins and there were numerous fires, but a great part of the city escaped destruction in that peculiar way of disasters, where one building will collapse while the one next to it remains upright and intact. One home will fall into a pile of broken timber or bricks while others keep their integrity. Many freeway overpasses had collapsed and others were impassable due to cracks and dirt slides. The epicenter was near the San Andreas Fault, with Palmdale the real focus of the damage. It measured 7.3 on the Richter scale, a pretty damn big earthquake by anyone's standards, big enough to shake Los Angles to its bones. Fortunately, the reservoirs held up. There was heavy loss of life but no-one knew the number of dead and injured for days. There were estimates, ranging from near a thousand to as many as five thousand casualties, most of them from fallen office and apartment buildings or on the freeways. The nation has suffered worse calamities, but it was bad enough.

I finally turned the television off at three in the morning and insisted that we all try to get some sleep. There was nothing else we could do then anyway. A few days later Amanda's sister Lorraine finally called. She had some cuts and bruises but otherwise was okay. Robyn's boyfriend got in touch. Their apartment building was still standing but had been evacuated. He was no longer laughing. One of my old friends who'd come through the war with me died when a gas line exploded but the rest of the people we knew out there survived. FEMA moved in and the National Guard was called up. Order was restored and reconstruction began, with the freeways getting top priority. Southern California would come to a dead halt without their freeways.

Three weeks after the quake, Danny called and told Robyn he had found a place for them to live. When she told us she was going to return, I thought about her rock. "Do you want to take your rock with you, sweetheart?"

She thought for a moment then shook her head. "No, I think I'd rather leave it here if you and Grannie don't mind."

It was fine with us. She left the next day and we thought that was the end of it. Instead, it was just the beginning.

I should have known investigative reporters would begin sniffing around sooner or later, given the number of people the three of us had called or e-mailed, telling them not only the day but the exact time of the earthquake. I don't know who gave out our phone number and address, but it really doesn't matter. Once we gave the warnings, a few hungry reporters were bound to have tracked us down. The first ones showed up right after Robyn left for California. It was a team, a female reporter with her male companion toting the heavy equipment.

I opened the door to a bright light shining in my face and the woman asking me how I'd known of the impending quake. No preliminaries, no introduction. If they hadn't been so rude I might have invited them in before realizing what they were after. As it was, I said a dirty word and shut the door in their faces. In the meantime, Amanda was on the phone, having a conversation with a talk radio host. She didn't realize it was being recorded until the next day one of her friends called asking her if it was true we'd predicted the earthquake out west. After comparing notes, we made a vow not to speak to anyone about the circumstances of the prediction. We never mentioned Robyn's name at all, but they found her anyway.

I turned away another television team later in the day and finally took the phone off the hook that night so we could get some sleep. I woke up to the catchy old music of *The Bandera Waltz* ringing my cell phone early the next morning. It was Robyn.

"Hi baby doll. How are things out yonder?" I asked.

She chuckled over the "baby doll" bit the same as she did with all the other pet names we had been calling her since she was a child, but then she got serious. "Grandpa, may I come see you again?"

"Sure, sweetheart, you can visit us any time, you know that. What's wrong, the media bothering you?" I didn't mention all the calls and visits we had been getting.

"Oh, yes, they're thicker than fleas on a hound dog but Danny and I are staying with some friends now. I think we've shook them for the time being."

I interrupted her by laughing at the metaphor, one that I used a lot. She let me have my fun, but got right back to why she had called. "Grandpa, I feel like I need to come back to Texas again."

"Is it like the last time or do you just want to leave there for a while? Either way, you know we'd love to have you."

"It's like the last time," she admitted, knowing exactly what I meant.

"Come on," I said, then had a sudden thought. "How are you fixed for money?"

"Well ... I'm running a little low, Grandpa. I haven't worked since the earthquake. Could you loan me the air fare?"

"Don't worry about it, sweetheart. Here, let me give you my American Express number. Charge your ticket with it."

She thanked me and took the number, including the little four digit security code. I told her to rent a car when she got to Houston. She thanked me for that, too and said she'd see us soon.

Amanda had been listening. She sat up on the side of the bed, looking pensive. "You know, I worry about that girl living out there by herself with all this going on."

I knew what she meant. "Well, me too, but she is living with a man."

"Oh, pooh. They're both too young to understand how the world works. If she makes another prediction and it comes true, there's no telling what kind of kooks and charlatans will start showing up on their doorstep. She'll never have any peace and it might even get to be dangerous for her. She ought to stay here with us for a while."

I agreed, but it's hard to get young people to listen to advice like that. She and Danny just didn't have enough experience under their belts to realize how Robyn could be exploited and, as Amanda said, possibly put into danger. "I'll ask her when she gets here, but if she agrees to stay, we'll probably have to take her boyfriend in the bargain."

That gave Mandy pause for thought, but didn't deter her. "We haven't met him. Maybe he's a good boy. I don't really like to see girls her age living with their male friends, but I guess it's the way things are these days. If that's what it takes to keep her here, I won't object."

I agreed with that, too, but we were both smart enough to know we weren't going to change the cultural environment youngsters were exposed to now. Each generation sets their own rules and makes their own mistakes, but eventually it will be those same kids who will be running the world. They'll probably wind up doing a pretty fair job, too, despite the older generation's reservations.

While I was musing over Robyn's predicament and how the world had changed since Mandy and I were that age, I wondered whether our only child, Jennie, had been bothered. Probably not. After the divorce she'd gone back to work for the State Department in the diplomatic service. She was in China right now, a senior secretary at our embassy in Beijing. Amanda and I, and Robyn, were far easier pickings for the snoops than Jennie. I doubted they had found Gretchen, either. She and her husband were living in Canada, working for one of the oil companies exploiting the tar sands in Alberta.

Robyn arrived early the next morning. She called us on the way from the airport in Houston so the coffee was fresh when she arrived. She didn't look quite as upset as the last time, sort of knowing what to expect now. She even put her suitcase away and called Danny to let him know she had arrived safely. She noticed her battery was low and took it into the bedroom. She came back and had some coffee with us, but I knew she was just being polite. Her eyes kept straying toward the rock, in its customary spot on the shelf by the fireplace.

I nodded my head in that direction. "Go ahead, baby. You're going to die of frustration if you don't find out what's happening this time."

She stood up, took a deep breath and walked over to the fireplace. She reached and picked up the rock before she could change her mind. Again, her face took on that blank expression, like she was off in another world. Perhaps she was, come to think of it.

But she didn't panic. She replaced the rock and came back over to the couch and sat down between Amanda and I, just like last time.

"Grandpa, could I have some brandy in my coffee again? Please?"

"Sure, sweetie. I'll get it. Mandy?"

She nodded. I brought in the carafe of coffee and the bottle and filled the mugs, one shot of brandy in each and the rest good Columbian coffee. I haven't had a drink that early in the morning in ages, but like Robyn, I thought it was justified.

Robyn sipped gratefully a few times, then set the mug down. "There's going to be a bus accident on one of those Reno Charter trips Saturday. Two couples we know are going to be on the bus. I'd better call. May I use your phone? Mine needs to be charged."

"Sure. Are they good friends?" I asked over my shoulder as I fetched our phone.

"Pretty good. We hang out together a lot. Danny wanted to go, but I was scared I'd be recognized and all the gamblers start asking me what to bet on."

See what I said before? Robyn was a very level headed girl. Already, she was thinking of the implications of her unwanted notoriety.

The first call went through. She talked for several minutes, trying to dissuade her friends from taking the trip. Her face was bleak when she hung up.

"I take it they didn't believe you," I said.

"Margo said they'd already paid for the trip and couldn't get their money back. And I don't know if they'll get hurt or not. I just know the bus driver is going to fall asleep and go off the highway and down into a ravine."

"It won't happen until tomorrow. Try them again in the morning. Maybe they'll think about it and change their minds."

"I will, Grandpa. Let me call Susan and Jantz."

They weren't home. She left a message, telling them what was going to happen and left our number and her cell phone number both on the recording.

Notice that I said she told them what was going to happen. No qualifications, just a flat out statement. I found myself believing her utterly. I was just glad she was trying to be calm about it this time.

Her friend Susan got in touch with her the next morning. Robyn repeated her warning. She told us that Susan and Jantz said they would "think about it". "Maybe they won't go," she murmured, talking to herself as much as us. Before doing anything else, she called Margo again and got essentially the same response. She sighed and looked helplessly at us. I knew she wanted us to tell her what else she could do to avert the disaster.

"Do you know the name of the bus tour company?" I asked.

"Oh!" she exclaimed. "Sure. But ... Grandpa, would you mind notifying them instead of me? You can tell them it was me who says it's going to happen, but maybe they'll listen to you quicker than they would if I called."

"I'll try." I got the number from the operator and after passing through one of those silly phone menus, I finally got to speak to a live person. I went about it in a roundabout way, simply telling the woman who arranged the trips that the driver of the bus leaving that morning was going to be sleepy and would have a wreck if they didn't relieve him and put another driver in his place.

The woman wanted to know who I was and how I got this information and so many other details that I finally just told her I had warned them and whatever happened was on their shoulders now. That quieted her for a moment but then she went right back to asking questions. I gave up and told her who the warning had come from. I guess she was one of those people who never follow the news or read a paper. She had obviously not heard about Robyn. She hung up and refused to accept any more calls.

I spread my hands and shrugged. "I'm sorry, baby. She just wouldn't listen unless I told her who I was and how I knew, but I guess she hadn't heard about you predicting the earthquake. Now they won't talk to me at all."

Robyn beat her fist on her thigh a couple of times. She sighed and leaned back, relaxing her body. "I guess it's just as well. I don't think I could stand much of that publicity again, but I'll call my friends back and ask them to try sitting up front and watching the driver if they insist on going. Maybe that will help."

She did, getting both couples on their cell phones. They assured her they would watch the driver and make sure he didn't fall asleep.

"That's all we can do. Let's have some breakfast while we're waiting," Amanda said. She set her cup down and got busy in the kitchen while I fired up my pipe and shared the morning paper with Robyn. I love to see young people read. So many of them today are visually oriented, such passive recipients of entertainment and information coming to them through the ubiquitous monitors and screens and hand held devices that they have no conception of how much more information can be conveyed by the printed word. Or how much more of their minds and imagination they use reading a good book instead of watching a movie.

After breakfast, I turned the television on and left it tuned to CNN news.

A full hour beyond the time Robyn predicted the accident would occur we were still sitting together on the couch. When I glanced at Robyn I could tell she was hoping she had been wrong this time. It wasn't to be though. At the top of the hour, the story broke.

Details were scanty at first, but a helicopter news crew got some overhead footage of the bus, resting on its side at the bottom of a shrub covered ravine. The front end was crumpled as if a giant had rammed it forcefully into the earth. A few figures were lying around the wreck but only one or two were moving. I put my arm around Robyn as soon as I saw the smashed front of the bus. In retrospect, asking her friends to sit up there had been bad advice. She had both her fists doubled, one on each side of her chin. Her eyes were wide open and staring at the scene, mesmerized by the sight of the wreckage.

On the far wall of the ravine, I spotted a rescue team rappelling down the side on ropes anchored to a big boulder. Another chopper came into view, probably a Nevada State

Patrol machine because the news chopper was forced to back off.

We followed the story periodically throughout the day. It wasn't good. There had been only six or seven survivors out of fifty some odd people on the bus but names weren't being released yet. We had no idea whether any of the survivors were Robyn's friends. They had evidently passed on the warning to others though, and that woman at the office of the tour company had recorded our conversation. It wasn't reporters who visited us first; it was the FBI.

The three of us were questioned for several hours while swarms of reporters flocked around our formerly quiet retirement home near Lake Livingston. I was allowed to call our attorney and the agents also let me contact the security firm who guarded our home when we were away. I was glad then that Amanda and I had quite a bit of money tucked away. We had done quite well with our software company and sold it for more money than I could have earned in twenty lifetimes at a regular job. I had the security firm run everyone off our property, the whole hundred acres, and set up a twenty four hour guard around the place.

It was fortunate for us that the FBI SAIC, the special agent in charge, was a news junkie who went in for the odd and paranormal. He knew all about Robyn's former prediction of the earthquake that had happened right on the money, just as she said it would. His knowledge probably saved us from being arrested on suspicion of terrorism, even though we would certainly have been freed in a day or two. A thorough investigation by the Federal Highway Administration found nothing untoward about the accident. It was ultimately blamed on the overworked bus driver. The company paid a big fine and the lawyers rubbed their hands together and began filing lawsuits by the dozen. That was later, though. The days right after the accident were the most trying, especially for Robyn.

Susan was the only one of her friends who survived. She wasn't even hurt very badly, just cuts and bruises, a broken arm and a bruised spleen that kept her in the hospital until the doctors were certain she wasn't bleeding internally. She sure didn't do Robyn any favors by spreading the tale around though, making her sound like the seer of the century, an envoy from God and the best thing to happen to America since the invention of sliced bread, all rolled into one. After I hired a secretary to screen our phone calls, Robyn finally talked to her, but it was the last time. She never returned to California. Jennie called from China, wanting to know what in hell was going on. Robyn and Mandy both talked to her, finally assuring her that there was no danger involved in all the hoopla; it was just a major inconvenience.

What about Robyn's Rock? Somehow we managed to keep that a secret. Robyn was smart enough not to mention it when talking to the FBI nor at the one news conference we allowed, with her permission. She attributed her predictions to sudden "visions", as I suggested and stuck firmly to that story.

The reporters hung around just outside our gate, tying up traffic until the highway patrol told them to move on. Then one of our idiot neighbors rented some space on his farm to a coalition of news media and it seemed as if some of them were going to camp there permanently, waiting on one of us to leave the confines of our property. I hired a local high school boy and girl to do our shopping, including some clothes and feminine things for Robyn. She fixed one of the guest rooms up real nice after we assured her that she wasn't imposing on us. In fact, Mandy and I both liked having her around. The thing was, I knew Robyn was going to get awfully lonely living out here, with nothing but the phone and internet to connect her to the outside world and no one to talk to except us old folks.

And then Danny showed up. With an agent, of all things—and not an FBI agent.

He stayed three days. I ordered the agent off the place as soon as Robyn told me she didn't want to talk to her. That caused a big row with Danny. It was behind closed doors, but I heard enough of it to burn my ears.

"Don't you understand, Danny? I don't *want* any publicity! Those reporters and kooks and nuts have about driven me crazy already."

He mumbled something I didn't quite get about money.

"I don't want any money if that's the way I have to make it! Can't you understand how horrible I feel when I know something bad is going to happen and no one listens?"

"They will now!" I heard that distinctly.

Robyn said something else but it was indecipherable. Besides, I felt guilty about the unintended eavesdropping already. I took Amanda's hand and we stepped outside to the big covered porch where we spend a lot of time these days when the weather's good. I could hear faint noises coming from the carnival-like atmosphere over at my neighbor's place. I remembered thinking he must have franchised some fast food booths and portable buildings for the crowds of media people and their hangers-on and gawkers. Amanda and I smiled thinly at each other. It wasn't nearly as peaceful out here as it used to be.

Three days after Danny arrived, Robyn came into the living room, looking grim and trailed by Danny whose handsome face wore an expression of disgust that brought out the unsavory parts of his personality.

She pointed an imperative finger at him and said "Grandpa, I want you to make Danny leave. I don't want him here anymore."

That was fine with me, and I was certain Amanda would have no objections. She had already expressed her dislike for the boy privately to me.

"Where in hell do you expect me to go?" the young man shouted. "I spent my last dime getting out here, trying to make some money for you and this is the thanks I get!" He said nothing at all about what he expected to earn off Robyn himself.

I spoke directly to him. "Son, if Robyn says she doesn't want you here, you'll have to leave. Sorry, but that's the way it is."

"Didn't you hear me?" he said sullenly. "I don't have any money. How do you expect me to go anywhere?"

Robyn looked appealingly at me. I turned to face Amanda. She nodded at me and went to fetch the checkbook. I wrote the boy a check for a thousand dollars and handed it to him. "The bank in Coldwell is open until three. I suggest you pack your bags and get on your way. I suspect any of those idiots hanging around across the road would be glad to give you a ride into town."

He took the check and started for Robyn's room.

"Just a minute, son."

"What?"

"I don't want to hear any slander about my granddaughter or any stories that aren't true right down to the last detail. *Comprende*?"

He didn't answer but I think I got my point across. A half hour later he was gone.

Robyn came back from closing the door behind him and collapsed on the couch. "I'm sorry for causing you and Grannie all this trouble and costing you so much money. I was almost tempted to let that agent Danny brought give me some money so I could pay you back."

"Don't you even think of doing anything that silly, young lady," Amanda said, speaking sternly. "You do and I'll get the fly swatter after you."

Robyn giggled, her face brightening into a happier expression than I'd seen for days. When she was a child and we baby sat for Jennie and Ron, Mandy used little love taps on her behind with a fly swatter to discipline her, never hard enough to hurt or even kill a fly, for that matter.

When Danny left, it solved one problem, but Robyn living out here by herself with just us old folks for company still worried me. Young people need to associate with their own age group, not old fogies like us, much as we enjoyed having her around.

Two days later, one afternoon while we were all relaxed after lunch and reading, Robyn suddenly put down her book. "Oh, no! Not again!"

It was Robyn's Rock, calling for attention.

Robyn stared across the room at the shelf where her rock lay, plainly not wanting to answer the summons this time. She knew, and we knew it was going to show her another calamity. "I don't want to touch that rock again," she said.

"Then don't," I advised.

She kept her attention glued to her rock even while she spoke to us. "But ... but what if something bad is going to happen to people I know, like the last two times. What if I don't touch it then someone dear to us dies and I could have prevented it, maybe?"

It beat me. "Mandy?"

"I think she's right, Justin. She wouldn't be able to live with herself. But you're a smart man. I want you to start thinking of some way to stop this."

I had already been doing a little of that. I had thought of simply taking the rock and throwing it out in the pasture or dropping it into the old cattle pond that was all scummy and overgrown with lily pads. No one would ever find it. Yet something prevented me from doing that. First off, it wasn't my rock. It was Robyn's. And second, I was scared of what might ensue if I did. Strange enough things were happening already. I didn't want to chance making them worse.

Robyn stood up and approached the shelf slowly, like a condemned felon taking those last few fatal steps to the execution chamber. While she was doing that, I got out the brandy and Amanda started a fresh pot of coffee brewing. I was going to turn her into an alcoholic if this kept up, addicted to Café Royal.

She held the rock only a minute or two, then came back and sat down beside me. I took her hand while we waited for Mandy to bring the coffee and our mugs. I was barely able to contain my curiosity.

Once we were all settled back and had taken a few sips of our brandy-laced coffee, Robyn told us what would happen this time.

"It's going to be right here. Someone I used to know is going to shoot up the high school where I went when we were living in Coldwell. Some people are going to be killed."

"Surely the authorities will believe her this time," Amanda said.

"Do you know when it's going to happen, honey? Or who the shooter is?"

She shook her head. "No, not who it is and I don't know the time. I just know it's someone I knew from back then and I know it's going to happen during final exams."

"Probably he hasn't made up his mind yet," I mused out loud.

"It's not a *he*. It's a *she*."

"Oh, Lord!" Amanda exclaimed. "Heaven help us. Justin, you're just going to have to make sure that school is closed down."

I rubbed my chin, then remembered I didn't have my pipe going. While I tamped tobacco I tried to decide the best way of going about warning the school board or the principal and her staff. It was going to be a hard sell, I knew that. Not when

Robyn couldn't say who would be doing the shooting or when it would happen, other than during Finals Week, which was due to start … I checked my mental calendar. Eight days from today.

"Grandpa?"

"Oh. Sorry, I was thinking." I blew out some smoke and watched it curl into the gentle air currents of the room and slowly dissipate. "I know some of the school board members. I guess that's the best place to start. But we'd better notify the police and FBI as well.

No one can say we didn't do everything within our power to have the school closed, but it was hopeless with such scant information as Robyn could give them, even after hours of exhaustive questioning. It was a large school, almost two thousand students. When Robyn had been attending five or more years ago, there had been almost that many, with slightly more than half the students female if normal ratios held true. And hell, it didn't even have to be a former student. It could be one of her old teachers or a shop owner or someone from Jennie's church or … it was useless to speculate. It could be almost anyone.

The authorities did what they thought best, not what I thought they should do. They were certainly wary of not acting at all, not after Robyn's other forecasts. First, they did close the school for three days, Friday, Saturday and Sunday. While the doors were locked to outsiders, the most thorough search that old building had ever gone through took place. Every possible nook and cranny where weapons might be hidden was searched by trained personnel. Dogs were brought in that had been trained to sniff out the oily metallic odor of guns or the ingredients of explosives. While the search was taking place, metal detectors and X-Ray machines were set up at every entrance, even the loading docks in back. At least three armed guards were posted by every detector. Temporary privacy booths were also erected so students could be patted down even after passing the detectors. In short, every possible precaution was taken at the school.

Meanwhile, a plethora of agents, drawn from the FBI, DEA, ATF and the Federal Marshall Force roamed Coldwell and its environs, questioning present and former students, janitors, teachers, food service employees and anyone else who could possibly have known Robyn. You'd think with all that activity, every single base was covered as tight as a stretched drum. At any rate, I had done all I could and Robyn still had no idea of exactly when the shooting would occur or who would do it, so I turned my thoughts to what my wife had ordered me to do. *Find some way to stop this!*

Okay, I was willing, but how? Analyze the problem first, I told myself, then you can think of getting your granddaughter out of her predicament. The first step in an analysis is breaking the problem down into parts. Separate the parts into what you understand and what you don't. That didn't take long. Did I know how Robyn was able to predict the future? No. Had something like this ever happened to anyone else? Probably. There were too many unexplained instances of dreams coming true; knowing someone has died while being a thousand miles away; that feeling of *Déjà vu* most of us have experienced at one time or another, and untold numbers of events happening that have no discernable explanation. How about mediums and psychic ability? Was there anything to either one? Nothing that's definitely been proven, and every medium thoroughly tested under controlled conditions has been revealed as a faker. How about Robyn's Rock? Has anyone else used an object as mundane as a rock to know the future? I had no idea, but I have never heard of such a thing. Most of the so-called psychics used crystal balls and exotic clothing and elaborate sets to fool their clients, those poor souls who want to believe so badly they'll pay good money to those charlatans. So start with the rock.

Robyn's Rock, a simple little rock she had picked up from our road, just one of a million other pieces of gravel laid down when I had our road overhauled and repaired. Why had Amanda and I saved it all these years? Probably because it reminded us of Robyn, how bright and questioning and cheerful she had been as a child, but mostly because she had been so taken with it, so fascinated by that little hunk of rock. And she had asked us to keep it for her. So start there. Have it analyzed, then see where we stand.

You don't get to be as old as I am without knowing a few important people here and there. I knew more than the average Joe, simply because we'd made a good living with computers. Amanda and I had both gotten our degrees a little later than most young people. We had to work our way through school, going one semester, working a semester, then starting back. I wound up with a degree in computer science, back when they first began changing the world, and later went on to obtain a Masters. Amanda majored in business. We took what little savings we had a few years after graduating and started our little company in the garage. It grew rapidly at first, almost too fast to keep up with, then business fell off almost as quickly during the dot.com bust. We dern near went broke back then but managed to hang on until times got better. Eventually we sold out and retired with quite a lot of money in stocks and bonds and cash and various other investments.

Computers are based on quantum mechanics. As crazy as the whole theory sounds when you try to explain it to laymen, it's been proven over and over again. I'm not a genius, but I'm no dummy, either. During the course of my business dealings I got to know a lot of scientists, some of them really smart men and women, much more intelligent than me. There were two in particular I wanted to talk to; Gene Lauderdale, a young man with a doctorate in chemistry and Mark Stemmons, a physicist specializing in quantum theory, one of the most brilliant scientists in America. I knew Mark pretty well. He lived and worked in Georgia. He talked like a pure redneck but looked like an aging movie star. If anyone could explain how Robyn's Rock worked, it would be him.

Why these two? Well I wanted Gene to analyze the rock and tell me what it was made of. After that, Mark was next in line. I had thought for years that if there was anything at all to psychic phenomena, then it had to somehow be tied to quantum mechanics, one way or another. I kept up with the sciences in a layman sort of way, reading the popular magazines like New Scientist, Discover, Scientific American and the like. The articles in them kept my mind busy and active and made me think a lot. The way I understood it, the whole universe, past and present, and every particle in it was connected through the quantum foam or Higgs Bosons or some other mechanism. Perhaps it was just pure thought that was responsible for the connection, with the observers actually creating the universe they observed in the strange system of quantum theory.

I settled on these two men and put in my calls. Both had heard of what I had been involved with and were curious as hell. Gene came to visit first, bringing a ton of scientific apparatus with him to measure Robyn's Rock backwards and forwards, top and bottom and everything in between. I made him come to us because I didn't intend to let that rock out of the house until we knew more about it.

Robyn was just as interested in the analysis as I was. It perked her up and took her mind off recent events as well as anything I could have thought of. She even proved to be a help to Gene after I got him set up in the garage where there were some 220 plugs. Robyn's degree was in chemistry with a minor in geology. They hit it off right from the start. After a few days I even thought I detected the beginning of a romantic interest between them, but before it got very far along, the shooting took place.

Damned if it didn't turn out to be one of the security agents who took part in the initial search of the school. Every day for those three days, she brought in automatic pistols and magazines of ammunition. She secreted them almost openly, in an unused desk in a closed off corner of one of the classrooms near the entrance she was assigned to search. It was located near the administrative offices, just the first set of restrooms. She volunteered to stay and help guard the school during that final week of exams. Fortuitously, she was assigned to the front entrance but it wouldn't have made much difference; she could have gone on to retrieve her stash of guns even if stationed at a rear entrance. The guards used the school bathrooms to relieve themselves when necessary and no-one thought a thing about it when she went inside. She bypassed the restrooms and went directly to the classroom where her weapons were stored. She motioned to the teacher from the doorway. When she came to see what the guard wanted, she told her someone had called in a report that perhaps a weapon was hidden in that particular room. Of course the teacher let her enter and of course she went directly to that unused desk. A minute later gunshots began ringing out, mingled with the screams of frightened students, the yelling of the outside guards who rushed inside and the moans of the wounded.

All of that was revealed by the teacher, who was shot but survived. Perhaps the guard, in her maddened, deranged frenzy took pity on her when she placed her bleeding body in front of a huddled group of sophomore students to protect them. The renegade official then went on to more rooms before the other officers tracked her down and killed her.

The shooter turned out to be a former student who'd been two grades ahead of Robyn but had known her well enough to double date with her once. Robyn remembered that night but couldn't recall any event or peculiarity of the woman that might have precipitated her madness later. Most likely there was none and the woman was suffering from undiagnosed schizophrenia. She had gone into police work and used the opportunity of a potential shooting at the high school to carry out plans she already had in motion. I know, that sounds like putting the cart before the horse, the effect before the cause, but that's how quantum theory works if you look at it from one angle.

Robyn was devastated, of course. For all her warnings, it turned out that it might have been the prediction had caused the event!

It took a lot of comforting to keep her on an even keel after that episode. Gene helped as much as anyone, assuring Robyn that sometimes a certain destiny can't be avoided. Personally, I think he was whistling in the dark, just trying to make her feel better. It did help, though. And the big surprise, at least for Gene, was that his analysis of the rock proved fruitless. It was very old, no doubt about that, but its appearance and constituents wouldn't fit it into a neat category such as quartz, unakite, agate, granite, flint, tiger's eye or any other specific type of stone. On the other hand, he could tell us that it was old, very, very old, and perhaps not even of earthly origin. It might have been formed somewhere else and came to earth later on as part a meteorite. It was impossible to say. Even so, I asked him to hang around until Mark arrived.

In the meantime, the media circus only got worse. I had to hire extra guards and another secretary to help with the phones and sort the mail that kept coming in ever increasing quantities. Most of it was either from cranks or fundamentalist religious types who stated positively that Robyn was a witch or an emissary from the Devil and should be burned, lynched or otherwise disposed of according to their interpretation of the gentle teachings of Christ. I never have understood how such types can reconcile that kind of madness with other Biblical wording. I instructed the secretaries not to give any of that mail to Robyn. She was unhappy enough without having to read threatening drivel from supposed Christians.

Mark arrived, white hair and lean body the perfect image of an aging male movie icon until he opened his mouth and dispelled the aura. He sounded like a redneck and even acted like one, asking where the beer was first thing after greeting Amanda and I and being introduced to Robyn. I knew him well enough to have had the high school boy get his dad to deliver a good supply. Mark liked beer as much as he did physics problems that would stymie almost anyone else in the world, the kind that took up pages and pages of indecipherable squiggles, the kind that lost me at about the second paragraph but made perfect sense to him.

We talked and joked while drinking, reminiscing over a couple of wild science fiction conventions we'd attended together back when I could almost match his beer consumption. He jollied Robyn and Gene about how close together they were sitting, then told a joke about little green men that I'd heard ages ago but was new to the young folks. Once everyone was relaxed, he asked for details.

I took him over and showed him the rock. He held it in his hand as if gauging its weight or texture then returned it to the shelf. He asked Gene a few questions about its age and composition. His eyes brightened with unadulterated interest when Gene told him it was older than the earth. Then he turned to Robyn.

"What do you feel when you're holding the rock and you have those visions? Can you describe it?"

"No, sir, not really. I go into sort of a trance for a minute or so, then suddenly it's like a scene appears in my mind, all in perfect detail." She shuddered, obviously remembering some aspects of the three incidents she's just as soon have forgotten.

"Don't call me sir. I'm too young for that." He grinned at her. "Okay, a trance, huh? Does the rock feel any different while you're having the visions?"

Robyn screwed up her face, thinking back. "You know, Doctor Stemmons, now that you mention it, I think it gets a little warmer those times. Does that mean anything?"

"Just call me Mark, Robyn. I'm not a formal guy. That doctor business is for the lab and lectures. And yeah, it might mean something." He shrugged. "And it might not." He drained his beer and stood up to get another but Amanda was already bringing it.

"Thanks, Mandy. Robyn, do you know anything at all about quantum theory?"

"Not really. I had a little of it in my last year when I took an advanced physics class to finish the science requirements for my degree, but mostly I just memorized what I needed to pass. It was a harder course than I anticipated."

"Do you recall finding the rock?"

"No. Grandpa told me I said it was pretty and that I liked it a lot, but I was just a little girl then."

"Uh-huh. Something must have drawn you to it, though. Let me think a minute."

Mark's "minutes" can turn into hours of silent cogitation, but he didn't take nearly that long with Robyn's Rock. Say about a beer and a half. He took out a pocket calculator of a type I didn't recognize and punched some numbers and squiggles into it toward the middle of his second beer's worth of reflection.

He glanced around the room at all of us and grinned. "Folks like to say I'm an expert in quantum theory and one of the few old boys in the world who understand it, but that's a canard. No one can really wrap their mind around quantum mechanics to that extent. It's just too damned counter-intuitive. Our minds are gonna have to evolve a bit further before we'll be able to get real a handle on the subject. Howsoever, I reckon y'all are all educated enough to have heard terms like quantum foam and quantum connection, huh?"

"Sure," Amanda said. "We read a couple of good books about it not too long ago. *Warp Speed* and *The Quantum Connection* weren't they honey?"

"Uh-huh. They're on the science fiction shelf in the den in case any of you haven't seen them."

"Okay, good. Now we've got a starting point," Mark continued. "And here's my thoughts for what they're worth, but if you tried to spend them, they probably wouldn't buy much more than a Coors with a Cocola for change."

That got a good laugh but he was just making fun of himself. Whatever he had to say was going to be worth a hell of a lot more than a Coors.

"I think that old rock, what y'all are calling Robyn's Rock really does belong to her. Kids as young as she was when she spotted it haven't had their minds warped by the boob tube or their environment yet. Their sweet l'il brains are still open to the world. That rock was old before our solar system was born, according to Gene.

"Part of the quantum foam that is the totality of the universe became locked in some of the molecules in the rock, probably way, way before the earth formed. It's been quiescent until thought activated it—Robyn's thought when she spotted the rock and picked it up. At that instant an active connection was created between her and the quantum reality of the universe. It remained just that until she was a grown woman, able to form mature thoughts and realize she was attuned to something back in Texas associated with you. As it turned out, it was the rock, of course. Now why does it happen only when a catastrophe is pending?" He sipped at his beer before continuing. "Probably the emotion associated with the event that's tied to her. Wouldn't work unless she had some kind of involvement in it, as she obviously did with the earthquake, her great aunt, her live-in boyfriend, so forth. The same as when the bus wreck was going to occur and that school shooting. She isn't really looking into the future, you know. In the quantum sense of reality, there is no past, present or future either. It's all part of the whole of reality, of the quantum connection. Perhaps the events are close to her emotions on the quantum scale. Maybe some other reason, or maybe no reason at all in the ultimate sense, and it's all just guesses.

"Possibly if it's something going to happen to those dearest to her, it can be prevented if she warns them. Perhaps not. I'm just a physicist, not God. Like I said, I think the rock still had a bit of the original quantum foam intertwined with it, so to speak, and Robyn's mind connected to it when she picked it up. Now don't ask me for a bunch of finicky details 'cause you don't have the math for it, and even if you did it still wouldn't mean much to you. Just think of the connection between Robyn and her rock as a statistically unlikely event. I mean *really* unlikely and improbable, but it happened just the same, catching them both at the exact perfect time. Maybe a fentosecond earlier or later, maybe not quite that quick, but might near, and her observation wouldn't have caused the connection between her and the part of the quantum reality that was activated. The rock would've been run over and mashed into the dirt and buried and probably never seen again until maybe a jillion years later. Or more likely, never again."

He paused to finish the can of beer he was working on. Amanda had another ready for him. He was really wound up and we were all listening to him as avidly as I remember me doing the first time I heard "Rock Around The Clock", one of the first great Rock and Roll hits back when I was barely into my teens.

"So now we have the connection, but Robyn forgets all about it. The Rock didn't though. It 'remembered' and you probably couldn't have gotten rid of it if you tried. It was locked to this old house and still connected to Robyn wherever she went because her observation *created* the connection.

"Then she grew up, of course, but remember the connection. Somehow, something triggered her awareness of it. It wouldn't have mattered if she were gone clean into the next galaxy, when the trigger was pulled. Distance doesn't have any meaning in the sense of quantum connections or quantum physics in general. It drew her back home because folks she knew had been placed in danger."

He stopped to get on the outside of some more beer. "You're probably asking why it happened now rather than sometime earlier or later. I can't really say, but probably it occurred the first time folks she was connected to, in the same old fashion we're all connected here, were put in harm's way. I suspect it was because her brain has just reached its full and highest peak of maturity. Not in the sense that she's had so much experience, but like her brain will never function quite as well again as it does now and for all practical purposes the next couple of years. She's just at the age when her brain is working in overdrive, in the most capable, skilled and proficient manner it ever has and ever will. The same holds true for all of us. Around about twenty five or so we reach our peak of creativity and reasoning power. After that, it's the experiences of our environment and the accumulation of knowledge that keeps the old brain cells pumping out ideas."

I was ready for some coffee to offset the beer, with maybe a half a jigger of brandy to go with it. Mandy sensed it and brought the bottle. I noticed it was almost empty. And it wasn't the same brand as what we'd been drinking lately. I doubt if I've had that much brandy since our last trip to Vegas when I got on a winning streak at blackjack and so long as I kept a brandy and coffee at my elbow I couldn't lose if I tried. I kept handing Mandy hundred dollar bills when she passed. She wasn't carrying her purse so by the time she drug my drunken body away from the blackjack table she looked as if she had gone from a C to a DD in one afternoon. I lost most of it back later but that's another story.

After I took a few sips and felt my mind settling back down from the overload of data I looked at Mark, wondering how that wonderful brain of his worked when he mixed beer and physics. I'd be willing to bet a lot of his synapses were smoking hot by then and he was using ethanol to cool them off, like an internal fan struggling to keep a computer from getting too hot.

Everyone else was staring at him, too, as if hypnotized. Especially Robyn, poor thing. She was probably wondering why it had happened to her, of all the people in the world. I saw her hand slide into Gene's. She leaned against his shoulder, wanting his closeness.

Trust Mandy to cut to the heart of the matter, like she usually does with a tough family problem. She eyed Mark with her big blue eyes, still the color of the sky on a bright summer day after all these years. "That's all very well, Mark. In fact, I'm sure it's about the best explanation we're ever likely to get, but it doesn't solve anything. What is our poor girl going to do? She can't live like this the rest of her life, hiding out from those damn snoopy reporters. They ought to be thrown in jail, damn them, harassing her day and night!" You could almost see sparks from the fire in her eyes. When Mandy says "damn", it's like anyone else cussing a blue streak.

Mark didn't flinch. Instead he grinned like the village idiot who'd just stepped in a pile of cow flop and was wiping it off on the front doorstep right where someone else would get it next. "I'm surprised none of you have thought of the most obvious solution. It's the simplest thing to do."

"Well, don't keep us in suspense. Spit it out." Amanda had her dander up. Mark had better hurry or she might serve his next beer on top of that pretty white hair.

He saw the look on her face. "Oh, okay. Why not have Robyn make about three or four false predictions in a row? Just as soon as the media hounds think she's no more accurate than any other of those wahoos that call themselves mediums, they'll forget all about her and go on to other stories, like a kitten up a tree or another politician caught with his mouth in the trough like the hogs they are."

Now why hadn't we thought of that? Too obvious, I guess, like not seeing your filing cabinet because the printer is sitting on top of it. And that's exactly what we did. It worked perfectly. The fourth time Robyn called the newspapers and television stations with an announcement of an impending calamity they wouldn't even speak to her because her last three predictions hadn't even come close.

That left only one problem. What was Robyn supposed to do when she felt her rock calling and she had another vision while holding it, something we all knew was as inevitable as the sunrise.

Mark had an answer for that, too. He made Robyn go over all three of the incidents she had predicted with such accuracy, probing for every little detail as she talked, and not allowing her to skip so much as what color blouse or pullover she was wearing each time. Part of that was just his method of being sure she hadn't omitted anything that might have had the least bit of importance. After the second telling he leaned back on the couch and refused Mandy's offer of another beer.

"No, I have to be going soon and I'm driving, remember? I need to sober up. Just let me ask Robyn one question."

She sat upright and clasped Gene's hand so tightly I saw him wince. "Go ahead, Mark."

"Tell me, after you gave all those warnings, how many lives do you think you saved?"

Her lips parted in surprise but no words came out. She rubbed her forehead and thought about it. "I don't think I saved anyone. In fact, I … I might have caused the death of my friends on the bus by asking them to … to sit up front and watch the driver." It was hard for her to say, but she got it out. A tear escaped and trickled down her cheek and dropped from her chin. A second one followed and then she was sobbing against Gene's chest while he made those little meaningless sounds of comfort. She cried for a long time, a much needed catharsis. Mandy leaned against my chest and cried with her. A tear or two escaped from my eyes and mingled with hers.

Robyn's Rock still sets in its honored place on the shelf by the fireplace, but she never touched it again, even when she felt an urge to do so. Curiously, the intensity of the compulsions faded the longer Robyn stayed near us. Finally they went away altogether.

Amanda and I deeded ten acres of our place to her. She and Gene built a nice little home, finishing it up just before the marriage.

More years have passed. Robyn has three children. She works from home. I don't think I've ever seen as happy a family as she and Gene and the kids. Our great grandchildren like to come and visit with Grannie and Grandpa. They call us that, just as Robyn still does. They're good kids, bright and cheerful, with the years stretching out in front of them like an endless road, filled with a boundless future. I had doubts during some periods of my life over what lay ahead, thinking the human race might actually destroy itself, but no longer. I can die peacefully now, secure in the knowledge that we're moving into space, ever more rapidly. Our eggs are no longer all in one basket.

There's only one thing that troubles me these days while Mandy and I live out our last few years. Gracie, Robyn's oldest child is six now. She comes over more often than the two younger ones. And sometimes she'll stand near the fireplace and stare for long, long minutes at Robyn's Rock. It makes me wonder what's going on in her mind and what she's going to do when she's grown. I hope she will leave Robyn's Rock there where it belongs, but there's no guarantee. There's never a guarantee of the future, not even when you're the one doing the observation. There's a multiplicity of possible histories and futures and which one happens depends on what we observe and think today. Robyn just went a little further than anyone else. Her thoughts combined with her observations and her connection to the quantum foam may have created what happened or even changed some parts of the events she predicted. That's why we all decided it's best to leave the future alone if we can. We're better off just waiting to see and hoping for the best.

THE END

Now you know why I hope the rest of the story is fiction. I just now went into the living room and over to the bookshelf that holds some of our knickknacks and had a look. Robyn's Rock is still there, all innocent-looking. I hope it stays that way.

The explanation for the following stuff is given in the introduction, just the way it was published online and with the same title. I don't write much humor any more. If you want to read other bits of silly stuff about our farm life and growing Christmas trees I invite you to purchase the collected stories in my two books, Life on Santa Claus Lane *and* Laughing All The Way.

A STEEL TRAP MIND & OTHER VIGNETTES

INTRODUCTION

During the last part of October of this year, 2006, we had a tremendous amount of rain over a period of a week, twenty inches or so. During much of that time the satellite for my computer couldn't be contacted so I wasn't able to get on line. Still, I can't stay away from my computer. I finished up my last novel, *Warp Point* then began looking through some old files I had kept that were in a different word processing program. I had never been able to access them before, but while fooling around, I finally found the right key. The result? I discovered a few of my long lost humorous stories, plus a little vignette on psi ability. They've never been published. All the material I found which I thought readers might enjoy is in the collection here. I have to admit, I got some laugh-out-loud responses from my wife, Betty. I also had to get her permission before publishing one story—but that's getting ahead of myself. Besides, if you're like me, you're wanting the author to quit babbling so you can get on with the reading. So here are the stories. I hope you enjoy them.

A STEEL TRAP MIND

A steel-trap mind is a wonderful thing to have and isn't given to just everybody so I'm happy that I've been blessed with one. Ever since I was young I've had a good memory. I still have, but I have to admit; nowadays it needs to be supplemented by a list or two. Just simple lists, mind you. That steel-trap mind of mine is still largely intact.

The other day I made a list for my day's activities. Go to the grocery store. Take off trash. Stop at post office and mail package. Come home. That last item really wasn't necessary but it never hurts to play it safe is what I always say. Before leaving, I looked at the list. Shucks, I thought, only four items. No sense cluttering up my pockets with a list of only four items. I left it laying on the counter.

As soon as I was finished going to the library to drop off a book, which I forgot because it wasn't on my list, although I swear I thought it was, I got my second item accomplished, which was to go by the bookstore where I bought a couple of books, but somehow didn't remember them as being the books I had originally intended to buy but they looked like pretty good reading so I bought them anyway. After that, of course I got a haircut, thus completing the three main items on my list. The fourth I remembered clearly, go home and I did, making only two wrong turns and forgetting that blasted new stop sign at the country road again, but fortunately the other drivers slowed down when they saw me coming. I'm sure they recognized the famous local author and Christmas tree farmer and wanted to get a good look at me is why they slowed down, no matter that when my wife Betty is with me, she tells me it's because they never know which way I'm going to turn, but I'm sure she's just kidding and I always ignore those kind of remarks.

Anyway, I got back home and was feeling proud of myself for remembering all the items on my list, then as soon as I got through the door Betty asked if I had remembered to mail her package. I said of course I did, wasn't it on the list? She said that's no guarantee when you leave your list. I remembered the list, I said. No you didn't, she said, I see the package right there on your desk.

Well shucks and other comments. At least I had remembered three items out of four, which is 90% correct in anybody's book. I went to put the package back on my list but couldn't find where I had put the list so I just made another list. I placed it on my desk and went to sit down except Betty asked where the grocery stuff was. I said what grocery stuff? The stuff on your list, dimwit, she said, which I don't think is any way to talk to your husband but never mind. Besides, I couldn't remember having any groceries on my list. I went to look.

Dern it, I couldn't find that list and I knew it was somewhere. I looked on my desk amongst the other stuff there; some accounts, some bills, a few CDs, two business card holders, some more bills and a package which I wondered why hadn't gotten mailed yet. I lifted the package, intending to show it to Betty and ask her what it was doing just sitting around, and I found a list under it. It had four items on it.

Take out compost. Go to grocery store. Ask Betty what she needs. Make a list.

I went and asked Betty where her grocery list was since I had plainly written on my list for her to make one. She told me she was going to the grocery store and would I please just take out the compost. I said sure, just let me get it on my list. She said why don't you just take it on out now and forget the list, which goes to show that women plainly don't understand the value of lists. I got a new tablet and wrote down "take out compost" and put the tablet down. I emptied my trash can from the office and thought, well, that takes care of that list, but then Betty hollered from the kitchen, what did you do with the grocery list? and I hollered back that I had the grocery store on my list and is that what she meant?

That obviously wasn't what she meant, so I started searching around for a grocery list. I found a list that told me to write a story about lists and other things in the bill basket and a list about doing some road repair and culling some trees and giving Biscuit a treat three times a day so I stopped whatever it was I was doing and ran to tend to the important business that was on that list while it was still on the list. I passed Betty and sat down to give Biscuit a treat. His treat bowl was empty which reminded me that somewhere I had made a note to fill it. I looked in the treat bowl and sure nuff, there was a list but it said something about groceries so I put it back until I could get to my main list which I remembered was to remind me to go to the grocery store.

Biscuit was sitting up and begging and my steel-trap mind remembered that it was about time for supper and he wanted to be included. I went to look for Betty to ask her what time she was going to feed me and Biscuit but all I found was a note which said "*gone to grocery store and don't forget to bring in some firewood*." I didn't want to forget that so I put it on a list. It seemed to me I had started a new list recently but I couldn't find it so I decided I hadn't and started another list reminding me to wash the pet food bowls. While I was at it, I put down go to the grocery store and take off the trash and especially to mail a package I had seen on my desk so I wouldn't forget and get Betty annoyed at me. There's nothing like a list to keep your activities straight.

Betty came back a little while later, mumbling to herself.

What's wrong? I asked.

I forgot to make the grocery list, she said and looked at me like she just dared me to say something. I wanted to tell her she ought not to forget to make a list of things she wanted to do, or wanted to get at the grocery store, because that's the only way to keep yourself organized when you get older but I didn't say anything, and didn't even put don't say anything on one of my lists because my steel trap would be sure to remember that one.

When I asked Betty what time supper would be ready she gave me a list. It had a bunch of groceries on it. I started to put them on a list but she handed me the car keys so I shoved the list in a back pocket and found a list already there that included going to the grocery store. I wondered where in heck it came from. I decided right then that maybe I shouldn't make quite so many lists, and on the way out the door to go to the garage and get the tires checked like Betty asked me to, I wrote down on a list not to make so many lists. I think I did anyway but it's hard to say since I couldn't find it on any list when I got back from the Vet with Biscuit. Neither one of us has understood yet why Betty started mumbling about grocery stores and zoomed off in the car, especially since as soon as she got gone I saw a grocery list she left laying there where her purse lives when it's not out spending money.

She ought to make a list so she could remember those things is what I think.

The End

THE FURNITURE FORMULA

Once upon a time there was a caveman named Ug.

One day his mate, Uga, said "I don't like the way the rocks are arranged in our cave. I want to change them around."

"No," Ug said.

"But they'll look better against the other wall," Uga said.

"No," Ug said. "They look fine where they are."

"Well, how about if I rub some charcoal from the fire on them and change their color?"

"No," said Ug. "They look fine the color they are."

"All right, but I've decided I'm going to sleep on the saber tooth tiger skin for a while. You can sleep on the bear skin by yourself."

Ug slept unhappily on the bear skin by himself for several days. Finally, he said, "All right, already, Uga. Go move the damn rocks, or color them with charcoal or whatever the hell else you want to do."

Uga moved the rocks and smeared charcoal on the rocks. Uga then moved back to the saber tooth tiger skin and slept with Ug.

Ug was happy again.

And that is why, ever since then, women have always been in charge of furniture in the house.

The End

I believe that story might actually be true.

GOLDEN YEARS

I used to think I had a steel trap mind, but now I think I almost have Alzheimer's. I say almost because I still have my memory—it's just confused. For instance, yesterday I took Biscuit with me in the truck to go mail some letters. I pulled up by the mailbox, rolled down the window, opened the lid and came to my senses only after stuffing the dog halfway into the mailbox. I looked for my boots yesterday after my nap. When I found them sitting by the dogfood bowl, I immediately went to the closet and let Biscuit out. Sometimes I forget the name of things and have to describe them indirectly for Betty to know what I'm referring to. Like, those sheets of white stuff you print letters on, or that thing that rings and you have to answer it. Of course it could be worse. I still know my name. It's Darrell something or other. I'll find out as soon as I look at my name on the keychain, after I fish them out of the trash where I intended to toss the junk mail. Golden years. Fooey!!

THE END

This was written years ago. It only gets worse.

WHY READ AN E-BOOK ON YOUR COMPUTER?

1. If it turns out to be no good you don't have to get up to go get another one. There are plenty more on the reader.

2. They don't cost much, so you have more money to spend on ice cream or beer.

3. If your laptop gets stolen, you can claim it was filled with a rare book collection and deduct it on your income tax.

4. Your cat and/or dog can't lay on the pages while you're trying to read.

5. You will be helping to support a starving author. Me.

The End

PSI ABILITY?

The most amazing thing happened today. First a backdrop: a couple of weeks ago I moved from my usual reading chair to the end of the new couch. It was fine except the couch arms are wide and by the time I made room for my wastebasket the lamp was a ways off and didn't give me enough light. Now, I promise I never said a word about this to Betty, but just turned it over in my mind. Then last night, or actually last thing this morning, I dreamed of a light stand to solve the problem. In fact, I dreamed of a six foot high brass pole, supported on a round brass base, with a thin white plastic cupola about a foot wide on top, and a place for the bulb in the middle of the cupola.

Okay that's the backdrop. Now this afternoon Betty and her sisters stopped at some big Garage sales on their way back from Mississippi, and for some reason Betty bought an *exact duplicate*, down to the finest detail, of what I had dreamed of this morning. She said something just told her to get it. I could hardly believe my eyes when she walked in the door with it in her hands.

Coincidence? Or Telepathy? Foreknowledge? I don't really believe in telepathy, prognostic dreams or the paranormal but how do you explain something like that? It is a mystery to us and I suppose it always will be.

Of course there's another explanation. Stories abound of married couples who seemingly "read each other's mind" all the time. We've done that before, starting to talk about the same thing at the same time and so forth. But having your dream answered? From a garage sale? The same day? That's pushing it.

I guess we'll never know, will we?

The End

ANOTHER FURNITURE FORMULA

We just bought a brand new couch and ottoman and they were delivered yesterday. The couch looks very good in its designated spot, which my wife Betty designated, except the spot is out of reach of the TV unless you are laying down. I can live with that, although I argued for a spot where I could watch television sitting up as well as laying down and therefore could also be available to read a book or so forth in the same place. Well, I suppose I could read a book there anyway, because Betty very graciously moved that end table which was an antique but ten feet high and therefore impossible to set a coffee cup on, and replaced it with one of normal height. I can't read a book without a cup of coffee by my side. But then, after fixing it so I could sit there and read, she refused to let me use the new ottoman in that space. When I asked her how I was supposed to read without having my feet propped up on the new ottoman, she said sorry, you can't use it there because it doesn't match the couch. I said I know that, I'm not so old that I can't tell blue from beige and what does that have to do with propping my feet up? She said never mind, just leave the new ottoman in front of your old chair because it matches there. I said, well, all right but it seems a shame to pay a zillion dollars for a new couch and almost a zillion dollars for a leather ottoman, then not be able to sit down and prop your feet on it and read a book. She said don't be silly, you can prop your feet on the coffee table. The coffee table she refers to is the one that is so heavy and hard it has sent generations of Bains and Wards to the emergency room, or if not that, sent them hopping around on one foot holding the other and crying bloody murder from stubbing a toe on it. I said that table is too hard to prop my feet on unless I'm wearing my work boots and you won't let me wear them in the house. She said I should get some hard house shoes then. I said I have some hard house shoes and I never wear them because they're too hard. By this time I am getting very confused, especially when I gave up on the new ottoman and tried to move the old ottoman in front of the new couch. I was told to get that thing back out in the office until the next trash run because there wasn't room in front of the new couch for an ottoman and a coffee table both and even if there was she wasn't going to have a patched up, duct-taped ottoman in front of her new couch no matter if it did look countrified and almost matched colors with the new couch. I said something under my breath about two ottomans would look better than one ottoman and a coffee table but she heard me anyway and that is why I am sitting on a kitchen chair out in the office wondering what went wrong. I thought we were going to have a nice new couch and ottoman to use but apparently it's not to use, but to look at unless you sit in an approved posture with your feet flat on the floor.

I have now derived a new mathematical formula to explain such happenings as described above: *Women + furniture = puzzled husbands.*

One day your grandkids will probably run across that formula in their math books and say, hey look, now I know why Dad and Mom are always arguing over where the couch should live and where the chairs and ottomans go.

The End

This letter is from when I was corresponding with a friend on New Year's Day. Or perhaps the day after. My memory of events around that time are still kind of fuzzy. Anyway, here's the letter to my friend:

THE JACK DANIELS BUG

By the subject heading, you may assume I imbibed on New Year's Eve last night just like you did. The only difference is that I used Jack Daniels instead of Wild Turkey. However, this morning it felt like a wild turkey was clawing around in my guts and trying to get out. It should have just made its way to the top of my head since there was a nice volcanic caldera there, the result of an explosion the first time I tried to sit up in bed. The turkey you mentioned went potty in my mouth several times before I could get to the bathroom, or perhaps it was a bunch of nasty little Jack Daniel's bugs. In fact, I think they both invited some friends in to help. Eventually I managed to get some coffee going and got some down. And up. And down. And up...

I took so many aspirin that what was left of my head was ringing. I took a half-dozen silly pills. They seemed appropriate since I have been told I sure acted silly last night and I don't mean dancing. To confound matters, the temperature started out at 31 degrees and eventually got all the way up to 31.5, necessitating a fire. Or at least being ordered to produce a fire. It was kind of hard to get the fire started because the matches kept shaking so bad they would go out. They sure make inferior products these days. I know, because Betty told me I ruined my new work shirt. Personally, I don't know how she managed to give me that Christmas card, the one telling me she is still crazy over me after 23 years, with a straight face. Perhaps she meant I was driving her crazy but I was in no shape for deep ruminations so I gave her the benefit of the doubt.

I squirted myself instead of Biscuit with his heartworm medicine. My hands just wouldn't hold still. That must have been some inferior Black Label to cause my hands to shake that much because I only drank a half liter of it. Or perhaps it was the bottle of White Zinfandel. Or the Eggnog before that. Or perhaps I was just cold from watching A & M get beat in the snow bowl at Shreveport.

Along about noon Betty baked some home-made bread and brought me an end piece with butter and plum butter. It went down, came halfway back up, went down, came a quarter of the way up then went down for the count. I have to admit I did go back to bed again to help it settle in rather than go off on an exploring trip.

My throat is raw and sore and I can hardly talk. Betty said it was because I yelled and cussed in my sleep all night long but I'm not sure I believe that; I sure didn't hear anything.

Sometime in the afternoon I managed to get the whiskers off my face, then I laid down on the couch rather than going back to bed. I was lying on my back, with Biscuit perched up on the top of the backrest. Suddenly he saw a crow in his yard and made a flying leap towards the door, using me for a bounce point. As I said, I was on my back and Biscuit hit a very sensitive portion of my anatomy. Actually two very sensitive parts of my anatomy and it felt like he landed with all four feet. If I screamed any louder during the night than I did then, it's no wonder Betty went off to the other bedroom sometime during the night. Being speared between the legs by a 20 pound dog necessitated another trip to bed.

As the day wore on I lost my voice, not that I was using it for much more than moaning and complaining anyway but I guess Betty was glad to have a little silence around the place.

For supper we are having black-eyed peas and cornbread and I think I will try to get on the outside of some of Betty's pralines. They are too good to go to waste.

I forgot to mention that I used up a whole bottle of eye drops with no noticeable improvement in their bloodshot appearance. That is just another example of inferior products on the market.

I sure am glad I have this new computer desk since I didn't have room to lay my head down on the old one and feel sorry for myself.

My voice came back enough to moan some more during the afternoon while waiting on supper. It didn't do a bit of good. I still hurt and my tummy still thinks my gullet has declared war on it. I think it's time to go back to bed again. After the black-eyed peas. And perhaps I will carry some Cherry-Vanilla ice cream to bed with me. Now that is a clear sign that I have passed the point of wanting to die and hoping it doesn't hurt as bad as my hangov--I mean that bug I caught that's making me feel so bad. Betty just read that last sentence. She said if I caught a bug it must have been swimming around in the Jack Daniel's bottle and bug or no bug we are going to see the folks in Jasper tomorrow.

I wonder if there's any of that stuff left? Maybe....

The End

Fortunately, I don't catch that bug any more.

The following is one of the few humor pieces I've written that Betty didn't particularly like. I haven't a clue as to why not. She did mention that she was never jailed over any checkbook errors during the six year period from the time her first husband died until she married me, but I suspect she was so pretty and nice and sweet that the policemen just didn't have the heart to put her in jail.

This is the story I had to get permission to publish, by the way.

MATH MADNESS

My wife Betty and I have a joint checking account. No, let me re-phrase that: Betty has a checking account with both our names on it. All I use it for is to pay bills twice a month—and once a month when we get our statement, attempt the Herculean feat of balancing it. Here is how a typical session goes.

We're sitting at home, Betty in her easy chair and me at a chair at the dining room table. I learned soon after we were married that in order to attempt to balance the checkbook, I would need to talk to her. Often.

"Sweetie," I say, "I'm missing check numbers 314, 327 and 333."

"That's nice."

"Missing checks. Not nice."

"Why not? If they're missing, we shouldn't have to worry about them."

"Yes," I say, "but what I meant is that those numbers are missing from the sequence in the checkbook."

"What's a sequence?"

"Um, never mind. Do you remember writing a check to Wal-Mart? Number 314 came right after that."

"Oh yes, I remember now."

"Well?"

"Well, I wrote a check right after that to someone."

"Do you remember who?"

"Not right offhand."

"Well, do you remember how much it was for?"

"Not exactly, but it wasn't for much, I don't think."

"Could you maybe estimate?"

"It was for either fifty or five hundred, I remember that much."

I remove myself from the dining room table to the kitchen cupboard and medicate myself with a shot of Jack Daniels Black Label. I'm no fanatic about numbers. I'm perfectly willing to estimate to the nearest dollar. Or five dollars. But five hundred is pushing it.

"Can you maybe estimate a little closer?" I ask.

"I'm sorry, I just don't remember. Is it important?"

"Well, not unless you mind visiting me in jail next month."

"Why would you be in jail for heaven's sake? Are you planning on doing something illegal?"

"Not yet, but we're not finished with the checkbook yet, either. Never mind, I'll split the difference."

I mark down $250.00 in the checkbook in place of the missing 314 and move on after pouring another shot. I start totaling figures then remember Betty mentioning something about an ATM machine a couple of days before. I look, but the transaction isn't on this statement.

"Honey, did you mark down how much money you got at the ATM?" I ask.

"No, why should I?"

"Because I need to know in order to at least halfway balance the checkbook."

"What does an ATM machine have to do with our checking account?"

I pour another shot of Jack Daniels, a double this time, and bring it back to the table.

"The ATM machine gives you money, but they subtract it from our checking account," I told my loving wife.

"Now, really, honey. How can a machine subtract anything from our checking account when I didn't even write a check? I just gave it my card and it gave me the money."

"But—never mind, take my word for it. Machines are clever these days."

"If you say so," Betty said with a disbelieving look on her face.

"I do. Would you happen to remember how much money you got?"

"Not really. Why don't you just look in my purse?"

I did, after tilting the shot glass to my mouth. Her purse held a dollar bill, a quarter and a few pennies.

"You only have a dollar. You must have gotten more than that," I say.

"Well, you're probably right. I must have spent it."

"Do you remember how much you spent?"

"No, but if I only have a dollar, please give me some more money."

I take out all my twenties and put them in Betty's purse. I take all the Jack Daniels in the shot glass and put it in myself. I go back to the checkbook. It is beginning to look a little blurry from staring at it so much. That has to be what's wrong, but I am determined to find out approximately how much money we have in the bank. I bring the checkbook over to Betty.

"Sweetheart," I say, "Can you tell me whether this is a four or a nine?" She has written a check to a furniture store that hasn't cleared yet. It is for either four hundred and sixty dollars or nine hundred and sixty dollars. I show it to her.

"I don't know. Maybe it's a nine."

"Maybe?"

"Or maybe a three. It's hard to tell."

"What did you buy?"

"Some furniture, I think."

"Shounds logical," I say. It looks like you wrote it to a furniture shtore."

"Except I haven't bought any furniture lately."

"I know. I bet you didn't put on your glasses when you wrote it, did you?"

"Well, of course not."

I wait. I wait some more. Betty offers nothing else.

"Okay I'll bite. Why wouldn't youse—I mean you—put on your glasshes to write a check?"

"Because I don't wear glasses in public, you know that."

"Of course," I say, heading for the kitchen cupboard again.

I return feeling a little better, even if I did miss the chair when I tried to sit down. After consultation, we decide the check was at least three hundred but no more than nine hundred. I split the difference. I continue totaling figures. Whoops. Here comes number 327. I put away another shot to fortify myself before asking about it.

"Shweetie, here we have a check missing after the one yoush wrote for Biscuit to the vet for a thousand—what!!!!"

Betty looked down at her writing in the checkbook.

"Hm. Must have put an extra zero in there. I think it was only a hundred. Or maybe it really was a thousand. He was pretty sick after eating that bedspread."

"He washn't that shick."

"Well, if he was, isn't he worth a thousand dollars?"

"That doesn't have anything to do with checkbooksh," I said.

"It does so! It's in there, isn't it?"

"Never mind. I'll split the differensh." I entered seven hundred dollars, figuring that was pretty close since my fingers didn't want to work the calculator very good for some reason. Too much writing in the checkbook, maybe.

"We're at number 333 now," I said.

Betty looked at me strangely. "When did our address get changed?"

"No, I mean check number 333."

"Are you still fooling with that silly checkbook?"

"Yesh. How about 333?"

"I think I voided that one."

"You did? Why?"

"Because it's bad luck to use three threes in a row."

"Well, why didn't you write it down?"

"I just told you! It's bad luck to use three threes!"

I went and got another shot and finished balancing.

"Are you finished balancing?" Betty asked.

"Unlessh there's something youse--I mean you—haven't told me."

"Oh, that reminds me—"

"Wait," I said. I brought the rest of the bottle in to the kitchen table. "Okay, now yoush can tell me."

"I just remembered. I was out of checks one day and got another book from the box."

I examined our bank statement again. The statement date was the 13th. "Did yoush do that after the thirteenth?"

"Let me think. Yes, I sure did."

"I don't shuppose you wrote them down anywhere, did yoush?"

"It was only a few. I didn't think it would matter."

I emptied the rest of the bottle and split the difference of whatever it was I was calculating. Then I got unsteadily to my feet.

"Where are you going?" Betty asked.

"Thish bottlsh empty. I'm going to get shome more before I finish balancing thish checkbooksh." I said.

Betty bailed me out of jail the next morning. She paid the bail with a check. Without putting on her glasses. As soon as I recovered from my hangover I went to our savings account, drew out five thousand dollars and deposited it into our checking account. I did not make an entry. I never have since. I just stuff a bunch of money into the checking account every month and hope it lasts. If not I can always go get some of that free money from the ATM.

The End

I remember what caused me to write this story. It had something to do with our sex life, something good. However, back when I first started writing I was instructed by Betty that the subject was off-limits so far as writing about it went. Sorry. You'll have to stay curious.

THE NAUGHTY BED

Craig Smith never imagined he'd see the day when he would be happy about his wife, Penny, dragging him along on a shopping trip, but it happened. He just didn't know he would wind up being glad at the time. She was looking for a new bed to replace the old one in the spare bedroom of their new house and insisted he come along. Grumbling to himself, he did so, thinking, *a bed is a bed is a bed and what does she need me for? She'll get what she wants anyway, and besides, we won't be sleeping on it; our guests will.* Beside his dislike of shopping, he was also missing the start of the Oklahoma and Texas match-up, all over a stupid bed they wouldn't even be using themselves. It wasn't fair, he thought for the dozenth time since leaving home, but he very carefully didn't allow Penny to see his chagrin. He loved his wife and liked to keep her happy.

The furniture store was one she picked from the telephone book, among only three others in the small little city of

Wellman, Oklahoma where they had recently moved, him to take over the Medical Laboratory at the City hospital and she to work at the same hospital as head nurse of the Male ward. Craig followed his wife inside. They were met by a chubby little salesman who bubbled over with so much good will and happiness it almost moved Craig to smile at him. Instead he glanced pointedly at his watch.

"I know, I know, you're missing the big game, aren't you sir? Well, let me help you and we'll get you back home in a hurry!"

"We're looking for a bed," Penny told him.

"Of course, of course. A bed! Just what any happy couple needs! And fortunately for you, we just got a new shipment in. Come right along and I'll just bet we find what you want right away!"

Craig certainly hoped so but he doubted the man's words. Penny took forever to pick out furniture. He caught a glimpse of a television set in a room they passed and slowed his steps, hoping to catch the score. Penny grabbed his hand and hurried him along. He sighed and let her have her way.

"Right here, right here!" the cheerful salesman said as he led them into an expansive display room with dozens of beds, small, medium, large and of various designs and prices. Craig groaned mentally at the wide selection, knowing Penny would look at every one of them.

The salesman spread his hands out in a gesture of good will, inviting their perusal of his beds, smiling all the time.

An hour later they were still there and the little salesman's smile had all but disappeared. What was left of it was pasted on his face like a bad drawing by an inept artist and Penny was making signs of getting ready to leave and explore the other stores in town.

In desperation, the chubby salesman plucked a brochure from his desk and opened it at random. "Wait, ma'am! This just came in. Maybe you can find something here we can order for you."

It was only politeness on Penny's part that made her even glance at the brochure. She looked at it, started to turn away, then looked again. Her eyes glazed and for the first time in their mutual shopping career, Penny managed to surprise Craig. She lifted her hand and pointed a finger at a bed displayed on the center page of the opened brochure. "We'll take this one. When can you have it delivered?"

He was astounded. Never, in more than twenty five years of marriage and innumerable shopping trips had Penny ever bought anything without seeing it first, much less a major item like a bed.

"What's that truck doing outside?" Penny asked. She got no answer. Craig was avidly watching the last quarter of the Texas/Oklahoma game. Oklahoma had the ball and was moving downfield. He didn't hear a word she said.

"Craig!"

"Huh? What is it?"

"There's a furniture truck outside, but we just got home and the salesman said it might take a couple of weeks for us to get our bed. He said he hadn't dealt with that company before."

"It must be a mistake. Tell them to go away." Craig never took his eyes off the game.

Penny threw up her hands and went to the door.

Craig never noticed as their new bed was trundled into the house and set up in the spare bedroom. He signed the invoice, wondering mildly why both of their signatures were needed but quickly forgot the matter. Now Texas had the ball.

"Are you ready to look at the bed now?" Penny asked. She avoided any hint of sarcasm. Her husband's fixation on the yearly Texas/Oklahoma football game was one of his few faults; that and being a news junkie with an abiding interest in world affairs, and she had learned to live with it. All in all, she was pleased with their marriage. The only fault she found in their lives was the way they had both gained weight as they aged past fifty and how their sex life was slowly dwindling down to nothing in tandem with their fading looks.

"Sure, sweetheart. Wow, what a game! Did you see Randall make that last touchdown? By God, he ought to get the Heisman for that run alone!" Craig got up and followed his wife into the spare bedroom.

The bed was just short of king sized, making Penny wonder now why she had ordered it. It would be hard to find sheets to fit it. It sat lower to the floor than most beds and the light blue headboard was in the peculiar shape of a narrow arc, the highest point rising only a foot above the mattress. On the other hand, there was something about the bed that was indefinable, yet vastly appealing, just as it had been when she saw its picture in the brochure. The bed seemed to fairly *sparkle*, livening up the whole room. Its radiance seemed to imbue her own body, making her toes tingle.

"Nice. I like it," Craig said, a rousing endorsement over his usual comments on new furniture. "What's that red button at the top of the headboard for?"

"Probably just a decoration."

"Huh. It's funny looking, all the same." He strode up to the bed and leaned over. He punched the button and stood up. His body began tingling. A surge of sexual energy coursed through him, more intense than he had felt for years. He turned back toward his wife. Penny was already unbuttoning her blouse.

"Hurry," she said. Her eyes glistened with desire.

Six hours later Craig was totally depleted and completely exhausted. Penny wasn't in much better shape. She felt somewhat like what she imagined a cowboy must after spending all day in the saddle without a break. Nevertheless, they both had never had such an exhilarating, pleasurable, exciting and completely satisfying experience in their whole lives.

"What happened?" Craig asked weakly.

"You punched that button," Penny said and smiled lovingly at her husband.

Craig laughed. "Well, let's not touch it again for at least a few hours. I don't think I'd live through it."

"Me either. God, I feel like I've lost fifteen pounds."

Craig scrutinized his wife's naked body. "You know, I think you actually have lost some weight. And you look fresher than you should after what we've been through."

"You, too, sweetheart. God, it has to be this bed. It did something to us when you punched that button."

"Well, it's no wonder we lost weight, the way we went at it, but sweetheart, I'd swear some of the lines in your face have disappeared, too." He remembered all the different ways they had tried it and couldn't think of any of them that hadn't been great. And other than being a little washed out, he *felt* great. In fact, if they didn't have to sleep and eat and tend to the other needs of their bodies, he thought he could stay in the bed a week. He told Penny so.

"I agree," she said, "but we have to go to work tomorrow."

"Let's call in sick. Tell 'em we have the flu."

It took very little persuasion for Penny to agree to the deception.

"Penny, we're getting younger." Craig had seen it happening over a period of two weeks but at first he hadn't believed it. Now there was little room left for doubt. Just a glance at the bedroom mirror (their regular bedroom) while the two of them were getting dressed left no doubt. He looked at his wife, standing with her bra dangling from one hand. She was every bit as slim and youthful as she had been in her early twenties. Her breasts stood out from her body like those of a teenager. Her profile was that of a woman who regularly worked to keep her figure, yet the only exercise either of them had had since the bed arrived was *in* the bed.

"Not getting younger. We *are* younger. Craig, what are we going to do?"

"What do you mean?"

"I've already been getting strange looks at work about my appearance, not to mention the comments I've heard. I've been passing it off to exercise and clean living but I don't think many people believe me anymore."

"Oh, yeah. Same here. Well, let's call in sick again and decide what we're going to do."

"We've already called in too many times. I think we'd better just quit while we think this over."

"Without any notice?"

"I'd rather us leave without notice than try answering any more questions. Just call and tell them our parents need us and we're leaving town. I sure don't want anyone nosing around and finding out about our bed."

"I wonder where that thing came from?" Penny asked rhetorically, not expecting her husband to answer. They had discussed the matter to death already with no better answer than perhaps it had somehow came from the future, probably by accident.

"And speaking of ... should we tell the folks?" Craig asked. "Or better yet, let them use the bed? You know both our parents are old and ailing."

Penny let a smile play across her face. "Do you think they'll be able to manage it?"

Craig shrugged. "All we can do is tell them about it. And I'll bet they'll be willing to try it as soon as they get a look at us!" He flexed his youthful muscles for emphasis.

"All right. Let's call a moving company and go back to Texas."

"I guess that's the best thing to do. Someone will start rumors about deals with the Devil if we don't leave."

Two months later, after a family discussion, Craig and Penny's parents sold their homes in Dallas and all three families bought adjoining homes in a new development from the proceeds. None of them were working. They were all living off savings while they discussed whether to try obtaining false documents to give them new identities. They all knew in their bones that if word of the miraculous bed ever got out, they would not only never know peace again, they would probably live very short lives. And the government or the underworld or any other old but politically or financially powerful person would see to it that their fabulous bed was confiscated. They had no idea whether the effects were permanent or not, but none of them wanted to take chances.

"It's a damn shame we have to live in the shadows like this," Craig remarked one morning over coffee. "Eventually, we're going to have to figure out a solution." It wasn't the first time by far that he had made that statement.

"We've got another problem," Penny said. "Liz and Deron are coming for a visit."

"Oh, crap. Couldn't you talk them out of it?" Craig didn't particularly care for Penny's sister Elizabeth and cared even less for his brother-in-law. He could see disaster on the horizon already.

"Not them. Liz is up in arms about the folks selling out and moving without telling them a thing about it."

"Our folks shouldn't have given out our address or phone number."

"That would have made it even worse, honey. You know Liz would have called the police when she couldn't contact them or us. And how about your brother? Sean and Betty will be coming around, too."

Penny didn't have to say anything else. Craig's younger brother was fat, bald and talkative. When he saw them, he would bedevil them until he was told how they had regained their youth, or more likely, hassle the folks into spilling the secret of the bed. Craig sighed in resignation. "Sweetheart, you're right. There's no getting away from it; we'll have to tell them. But you get Liz and Deron aside and give them a good talking to and I'll do the same for Sean and Betty. We'll have to impress on them just how dangerous it could be if they spill the beans."

"Let's tell them the government will confiscate the bed if it finds out, and throw us all into a dungeon for the rest of our lives," Penny said.

"It probably wouldn't be much of a lie," Craig commented bleakly.

If the Smith family's neighbors thought anything was strange about the comings and goings of the couples living on each side of them, or the frequent visits by other family members, nothing was said of it. Craig cautioned his brother and his in-laws to come and go late at night or during the day when they were sure their neighbors were all at work. And both he and Penny reiterated time after time the need for secrecy as they saw their siblings grow youthful, just as they and their parents had.

Craig was surprised that his brother managed to keep the secret under his belt—a much shorter belt now. He was even more surprised that he even began to develop a liking for Liz and Deron as they regained their youth. Deron was the one who developed a real sense of responsibility. He not only explained over and over to other members of the family how politics and financial power worked, gleaned from his position as an investigative reporter for *The New York Times,* he related stories of how men and women could be savaged and broken at the whim of those wielding shadowy, behind the scenes influence and control. Better yet, he was good at thinking of plausible answers to the inevitable questions and spread them among the family to use when needed. As time passed, money became somewhat of a problem, but by taking minimum wage jobs where background checks were casual or non-existent and by Deron's generosity with his own munificent salary, plus the formerly elderly parents' savings, they were getting along. In fact, they were getting along so well that Craig suggested an experiment.

"It's not permanent," Craig said to Penny one morning six months later. By dent of almost superhuman will power they had not gone into the room where the "Future Bed", as they now called it, was located.

"That's too bad. But maybe if we used it long enough..."

Craig shook his head. "Maybe, hon, but it'll take years for us to really know for sure. In the meantime, we've got a rough baseline, I think."

"How did you calculate it? I know I don't feel quite so youthful and energetic as I did when we started the no-bed regime, but it's not bad yet."

"I know, sweetheart, and you're still just as beautiful as ever. But have you weighed lately?"

Penny's smile at the compliment faded at the mention of weight. "Yes. I've gained five pounds in the last six months."

"And I've gained seven. Whereas our weight stayed the same until we stopped using the bed. Also, have you noticed one or two extra crow's feet around your eyes?"

"Yes, damn you!" But Penny laughed. It was hard to be upset over such a little thing when almost all of her restored youth was still present.

Craig laughed with her but then sobered. "It's all right sweetheart. I know how you feel. Anyway, as I was saying, I've got a rough baseline. Taking our age as the benchmark we started from and what we looked like before the bed, and adding all the little changes I've seen in the last six months since we stopped, I'd say the effects wear off at a rate of about six to one. For every month we weren't using the bed, we lost about six months of our regained youth. That's very rough, of course, and may vary for someone much older or much younger than us. But judging from our folks, it isn't a whole lot."

"So if someone took away our bed, it would still take a long while to get back to the way we looked before?"

"Uh-huh. And the way we felt. And speaking of, the bed isn't in use right now." Craig wiggled his eyebrows suggestively, drawing a laugh from his wife, but she was on her feet before he was and heading for the bedroom. The special bedroom.

"It sure didn't take long to restore what we'd lost, did it?" Penny remarked the next day.

"Nope. That's encouraging, too. And have you noticed? After anyone's used the bed for a while, the sessions don't last as long or have to be done so often. We only stayed in the bed three hours, where we used to spend six when we first started, and we're already almost back to where we were. That's encouraging."

"What does that mean?"

Craig shrugged. "I'm not real sure, except that it probably indicates that people in the future didn't spend all their time in bed! Well, one thing I can say for certain. This bed, by itself, could probably keep somewhere between fifty and a hundred people young if it were in continuous use. Maybe quite a few more. Remember, I said my calculations were rough. Or shucks, more than that if everyone would settle for partial youth instead of looking like teenagers the way we do."

"They sure invented a doozy of a way to keep themselves young in the future, didn't they?"

"I'll say. I wonder how far ahead of us it was when the bed was invented?"

"Who knows? If it is from the future."

"I don't know where else it could come from, even if it did have to be an accident of some kind for it to have gotten here. The technology is certainly far beyond our understanding. Anyway, let's just enjoy it and not worry about it."

"I can't help worrying, Craig. It's worked out fine so far, but sooner or later..."

She didn't have to complete her sentence. Craig knew as well as her that sooner or later the secret would have to come out, by accident if nothing more. Which reminded him—he thought it was about time for them all to move to another city, and perhaps not congregate quite so closely next time. Moving every so often, he thought, was just the price they were going to have to pay if they wanted to keep the bed for their exclusive use. Or to keep it at all, for that matter. His interest in politics and national and world affairs gave him an abiding distrust of politicians and high government officials.

Liz was in tears. "I was so worried when the school called and said Lonnie had been hurt that I didn't even think. Then I told them I was his mother and they ... oh, Lord, you should have seen the way the principal looked at me when the school nurse called him to her office. She didn't believe I was his mother and he certainly didn't."

Craig could see why. Liz looked not much older than her thirteen year old son herself.

"Then once I had said it, I didn't see any way of backing out. Deron had to finally come get us before they'd let Lonnie go and then they started giving me and him both strange looks." She began sobbing profusely.

Deron put an arm around her. "It's okay sweetheart. Maybe it'll blow over. Besides, we'll be moving next week anyway."

"Can you take Lonnie out of school now?" Craig asked.

"Not without causing even more questions, since I've already given them one withdrawal date." He pounded his fist into the palm of his other hand. "Damn. One more week and we would have been gone."

"It's all right. We all knew things like this were bound to happen. And as you say, maybe it'll blow over."

The child welfare people were on Liz and Deron's doorstep the next morning.

Craig and Penny didn't hear about it until later in the day, after Deron's lawyer had bailed them out of jail. He and Liz had been arrested on "suspicion of child endangerment".

Deron spoke rapidly, as if he might be re-arrested any time. "Craig, it's our fault and I don't know how we're going to explain anything that the authorities will believe. They arrested us because that damn school nurse and principal made up some wild stories about "experiments". He curled two fingers of each hand to demonstrate quotations. Hell, my own lawyer only halfway believes my appearance is a result of working out and hair restoration. And God only knows what's happening with Lonnie. They've got him in juvenile detention while they find some temporary foster parents. Can you believe it?"

"What can I do to help?"

"Craig, I don't think there's much you can do. The best thing for everyone is for you all to pick new names, decide where to meet, then take the bed in a U-Haul and get the hell out of the city."

"Deron, we can't just abandon you."

"You're not listening. There's nothing you can do. Just pack up and go. If we get out of this, we'll stay here so you can find us, but be damn careful. You know how the government is."

"Yeah. Okay, we'll get moving. Tell Liz we're sorry."

"I will. Good luck."

"Same for you and the rest, Craig. 'Bye."

Lonnie was the weakest link, of course. A thirteen year old boy, no matter how loyal to his parents has little defense against a coordinated and professional questioning procedure.

Believing the boy once he broke was something else again, especially since he wasn't completely knowledgeable of how the bed worked. He only knew that his parents and grandparents had become much younger looking after visiting them and sleeping in that bed—although he knew sleep wasn't all that went on. In fact, up until now he had been amused with his thoughts of what went on in that bedroom. The people questioning him didn't seem a bit amused, though, and were adamant in their statements that if he wanted to see his family again, he had to tell them everything that went on at home.

It was hard for the authorities to comprehend what they had even after putting all the information together. Then, like a pot slowly coming to a boil, they began to understand, and as if the boiling pot had been a signal, their net began a wider search for more and more details.

The salesman remembered the woman who had ordered the bed, but unaccountably, he couldn't locate the brochure he had ordered it from. He did remember the name of the company, though. "It was called *Future Beds*," he told the FBI agent with great readiness, "but I don't remember the phone number."

The agent's face became grim. He had his orders. "Maybe a little bouncing off the walls would help your memory."

"Please, sir! I really don't remember." The normally cheerful salesman felt his vision become blurry from incipient tears.

"Just a minute, Jim," the agent's partner said. "Mr. Smallman, have you ever been hypnotized?"

"No, sir. Never!" He thought perhaps they believed he had done something wrong while under a spell.

"Well, you're going to be. And pray you're a good subject. The Chief wants answers to this, and he wants them fast."

"The phone number's not in use, and the last time it was, a Mr. H. Jones had it," the psychiatrist told the agents.

"Could he be lying?" one of them asked.

"No, he's a remarkably extroverted and uncomplicated personality. He could have been lied *to*, perhaps."

"Come on, Jim. Let's go find Mr. H. Jones."

Mr. Herman Jones knew nothing about a bed, other than the one he slept on, a perfectly normal inexpensive queen sized bed such as could be found in a million other homes.

There was no such company by the name of *Future Beds*, either, not now. One such company had gone out of business years ago but that was all. The search widened, concentrating now on the Smiths and their relatives.

The families had split up, intending to meet in El Paso. Craig and Penny's parents were apprehended in Abilene and Midland, respectively, but one of them managed a phone call when they noticed a patrol car behind them.

Craig immediately changed directions and headed north, narrowly escaping detection in Amarillo, where Sean and Betty were picked up. By then, the story of the remarkable bed had made it to the highest levels. Craig and Penny really had no chance of remaining free for long, not with a nationwide, all-agency search for them underway. It came as they were making a run for Canada.

"There's a patrol car behind us, honey," Craig said to his wife, who was driving.

She shivered and slowed down.

"It's lights are flashing. I guess you better pull over."

"Maybe they just thought I was speeding," Penny said hopefully, but neither of them really believed it, especially when another patrol car crossed the divider and blocked them in front while the patrolmen in the rear jumped from their vehicle with guns drawn. Their long drive was over.

"Hi folks," Craig said, as he and Penny were escorted into a large conference room where all the rest of their family was waiting. Even Lonnie was there.

"Hi, Uncle Craig," he said. "They lied to me when they made me tell. They said Mom and Dad and gramps and grandma and ever'body else would go to jail for the rest of their lives if I didn't say what the bed did. I'm sorry, Uncle Craig."

"It's all right, Lonnie. You didn't do anything wrong. I'm just glad to see you're safe." He looked around the long table as he pulled one the comfortable wheeled chairs out for his wife and seated her, then sat down himself. He did his best to appear calm, but he couldn't help but worry over what was going to happen. Worst of all, he thought their happy times in the marvelous bed were over and that now their new found youth would slowly fade as politicians and billionaires and generals took it over for their own selfish use. Not but what he hadn't been selfish about it himself, but damn it, they had bought it fair and square and it belonged to *them*. Not that he thought that would make a difference.

A big man with heavy jowels and piercing dark eyes entered the room. The coat of his suit was opened so that the holstered automatic was in plain view as he moved. Two other men and a slight, rather pretty woman who appeared to be in her forties or thereabouts followed the first man inside. The four of them took empty chairs at the end of the table.

The jowly man's eyes roved the length of the conference table before he spoke. "None of you know me. In fact, you don't know any of us. If you have a memory for faces, I suggest you lose it. Am I being plain enough for you?"

"Now just a goddamned minute," Craig's father began, rising half out of the chair on Craig's right.

"Sit down, Pop. Let's find out where we are before getting all upset. It might not be as bad as we think." In his own mind, he thought it was very bad, but saw little need of passing his unease on to the others. Let the bad guys make the first move, then see if there was any way out.

"That's a very good attitude, Mr. Craig Smith. Now let's get our cards on the table. We know—we *know*—that the bed you bought in Wellman is responsible for making every one of you young again, except for the youngster, of course. We know, so don't try fooling us. What we *don't* know is how the fuck you do it. Pardon my language, ladies, but my boss is wanting answers, and he wants them fast. He's not a well man."

Craig rubbed his chin. "Is your boss who I think he is?" He knew, as did everyone else, that the president had recently suffered a heart attack.

"Possibly, but we wouldn't have him test something unknown first. We tried with some others. Am I correct in saying that the bed control is the red button on the headboard?"

Craig shrugged. "It works for us."

"Don't get smart. It *doesn't* work for anyone we've tried it on, and it's my understanding that results are apparent almost immediately. Is there a password or something else we're missing? And don't try lying. This room is wired and all your vital functions are being monitored."

Craig had already suspected that. Now he suddenly began wondering if the bed had been damaged in some way after it was taken from them. He was also wondering if he might have an advantage he didn't even know about yet if the bed wasn't working for anyone outside the family. Of course there was only one way to find out. "I don't know what's happening, but it seems to me the simplest thing would be for you to take my wife and I to the bed and see if it works for us."

"All we need is you."

"It takes two—or haven't you tried it yet?"

The big man had the grace to blush. He nodded to the woman. "Margaret, come with me and Mr. and Mrs. Smith. Jordan, you and Phil make the rest of them comfortable while we're gone."

"Craig, don't you know they'll be *watching* us?" Penny whispered to her husband.

"Yeah, and recording, too, I imagine," he responded, not bothering to lower his voice.

The bed had apparently been set up in another part of the building. As they were escorted along hallways, Craig noted the type of construction, the sort of portraits on walls in offices they passed where doors were ajar and put those together with the fact that they had been driven a long way in an automobile with tinted windows they hadn't been able to see out of, and that after a flight to a large city. Then he observed the deference paid to a certain type of persons and came up with the knowledge of where he thought they were.

"We're somewhere close to the White House," he said nonchalantly and watched the start of surprise on the jowly man's face. "In fact, I wouldn't be surprised if we weren't actually in the White House."

"Shut up," he was told.

"Oh, let it go. None of us are dummies, you know. In fact, you might get more cooperation if you treated us more like guests and less like prisoners."

"That's not my decision."

Craig shrugged and smiled at Penny. The man had just confirmed their location. Perhaps things were looking up.

"In here."

Craig and Penny were led through the outer alcove of a room, practically overflowing with mean looking marine guards. From there they were taken on inside. Their bed was in the next room, resplendent in new sheets and pillowcases of pale blue satin. Bedside stands held lamps and carafes of water. On another table, champagne was iced in a cooler with glasses beside it. A wet bar lived in one corner of the room and a dresser and sofa and chairs and various sized coffee tables were scattered around in an attractive arrangement with the bed as its centerpiece.

"Do you mind leaving us alone?" Craig asked.

"Yes. Start doing whatever you do to make the bed work."

"I won't do anything under duress and especially while you people are in the room with us," Penny stated firmly.

"Maybe a thumbscrew or two for your parents might make you more cooperative."

Penny glared daggers at the man and woman in turn. The petite woman was moved enough to blush but not enough to leave the room.

"This is under protest," Craig said, "and I hope to hell your boss sees all the recording." He stepped forward three long strides, bent over the bed and pressed the red button, then looked back at his wife.

She stood there, doing nothing, nor did he feel impelled to action.

Craig laughed. "I think our bed requires privacy to work. Interesting. We didn't know that ourselves."

It took another ten minutes of arguing and button pressing before the unnamed man and woman conceded defeat. They left the room.

"What's happening? Has it stopped working?" Penny asked, her face an expression of puzzled disappointment. Even with the prospect of being recorded having sex, she had unconsciously been anticipating it after being unable to use their bed while on the run.

"I don't know, sweetheart, but I think ... never mind. Let me try it again." He leaned over and pressed the red button. Immediately, he felt that welcome surge of sexual energy sweeping through his body and knew even before looking that Penny was feeling the exact same thing.

"It took four us hours that time," Penny said happily.

"Yeah, I guess that extra hour was catching up. Whew! I guess we'd better see if we have the energy to get dressed. I'm sure we'll be having company shortly."

Penny rose up and kissed Craig then swung her feet over the side of the bed. "But what happened, honey? Why didn't it work at first? And why didn't it work for those ... those other people."

Craig laughed. "I think I know, but we'll have to run some tests to be sure. Won't that be fun?"

She kissed him again. "Yes! If they let us."

"Oh, I think they will," Craig said. "If my theory is right, that is."

"What goddamned theory?" The jowly man said as he burst into the room.

Penny held her skirt up in front of herself. "Get out of here, you bastard!"

"Yes. Get out, then if you're nice, I may have some good news for your boss. Not you, though." Craig smiled malevolently at him.

Three weeks later there was no doubt. Their parents and siblings were freshly renewed and the president and first lady were feeling much better. Craig knew because they had met the president and discovered through trial and error that his and Penny's presence and *willingness* to use or share their bed was necessary before they or anyone else could use it effectively. Mr. Jowls, as they had called him, was no longer on the premises. Penny had spoken to the first lady and he was never seen again.

Craig was glad to see his wife and the rest of the family being well taken care of and allowed access to the bed on a regular rotation, as well as given very well appointed quarters to live in. They were happy enough, but Craig was ambitious. He asked for an appointment with President McMahon for him and Penny. It was granted almost immediately.

"Good afternoon, Craig, Penny. It's good to see you. How are you getting along in your new quarters?" He leaned across his desk in the oval office to shake hands with them.

"Very well, thank you sir. I'm glad to see you looking so well."

The president smiled. "Thanks to you and Penny. In fact, Judy would like to extend an invitation to you both to dine with us tonight. She's very grateful to you both, and I'm pleased to say she sincerely likes you. So do I for that matter. It's really amazing how that bed from the future works, isn't it?"

"Indeed it is, Mister President. I have no idea how Penny and I got so lucky."

"Perhaps because you were graceful enough to give up something you wanted to do to please your wife by accompanying her shopping, something we men don't take well to."

"Craig isn't bad, Mister President. He tries hard to please, even with shopping."

"Well, that's rather obvious. Now, I'm not trying to rush you off, but I assume you had some matters to discuss with me?"

"Yes, sir. I'm sure you've been told that it takes the concurrence of both Penny and I together, and the willingness on both our parts before the bed words, either for us or anyone else?"

"Indeed I have. And I may as well tell you, that as much as we're trying to keep this amazing bed and its effects under wraps, some of its effects other than, um, sexual have leaked out. As a consequence, I have a stack of requests on my desk for appointments with you and your bed. We're going to have to do something about them."

"Yes, sir. That's what I came to see you about. Penny and I don't mind sharing, but we want to be awfully sure that the persons we do share with are deserving. Not just a little deserving but so well thought of there's no question about granting them a session."

"Of course. My thoughts exactly."

"And in addition, Mister President, the United States has lots of problems, both here at home and overseas. Particularly overseas. The leaders of many nations we have issues with are rather intractable, aren't they?"

"Well, yes, I would have to say that's true."

"And most of them are either elderly, or ill in some fashion or other; in many cases they are both old and ill, along with their spouses and ... significant others, shall we say?"

President McMahon rubbed his chin. A thin smile slowly developed on his face as he caught the drift of Craig's conversation. "I do believe you've just justified your request for an appointment, Craig. Of course there's a lot of details that would have to be worked out."

"Certainly, Mr. President, but perhaps your briefing concerning me noted that I pay a great deal of attention to national and foreign affairs?"

"As a matter of fact it did. Why don't you let me have my aides draw up a list of world leaders and the ... problems ... which might be solved should they have sufficient incentive?"

Craig nodded. "That sounds like a good idea, Mr. President. Suppose we leave that for you to take care of, and then you could send me your conclusions and requests and let me study them. Where we agree, there won't be a problem. And in those areas where our views differ, I'm sure we can negotiate suitable compromises."

The president laughed out loud. "Craig, I like you. I really do. If I could do it without congress raising cain I'd make you secretary of state right now. As it is, I guess you'll have to work in the background."

"We'd prefer it that way, Mr. President," Penny said.

"I don't blame you in the least. The public part of this office is the most trying. Well, suppose we cut this short for now and Judy and I will see you tonight. My appointments secretary will let you know when it's time to review our first list of prospective recipients of benefits from the future bed— assuming they agree to what we ask of them, of course." He winked as he rose to personally escort them out of the oval office.

It took the White House press corps and the national media a few weeks to notice, but then they began writing about world leaders suddenly becoming very friendly toward the United States. Saudi Arabia abruptly cut the price of oil in half. Iran gave up its nuclear weapons program. China devalued its currency. A prominent politician decided not to run for president now or in the future. Several wars ended abruptly. Russia decided to get serious about disarmament.

It went on and on. Before many months passed, the United States was once again respected and envied on the world stage and it seemed that the president had but to invite a foreign dignitary and his wife to stay at the White House overnight than all problems with their respective nations began to be solved in a hurry.

President McMahon was re-elected. Craig, Penny and their family remained young. Many national and world leaders appeared healthy enough to stay in office a long time where previously they had been thought to be too old and frail to continue. The world settled down into a period of relative peace and prosperity such as it had not known in its long fractious history.

And Craig and Penny continued to be a happily married couple. But sometimes Craig woke in the middle of the night and he wondered. Had leaders in some future looked back over history and seen what it would take to cure the world of its many ills during its period of the most turmoil, war and strife, then sent the bed back to work its magic? And if so, why had they picked him and Penny? Was it because he was an amateur dabbler and reader of world affairs so that he could choose wisely, or had the bed landed in their hands purely by chance, through an accident which took place in the future, and with no plan at all behind it? He woke up and wondered but he was never able to decide which it was, or whether it happened for some other reason altogether. And then he would roll over and put his arm around Penny and drift back into a contented sleep, secure in the knowledge that the world was a much safer and saner place to live in these days.

The End

Ah, would that the world really be that sane and safe!

This is an expanded version of one of my favorite short stories, by the title of Samantha. It has about doubled in size with much new material.

SAMANTHA'S TALENT

Chapter One

Elaine Douglas was getting tired. She flicked the fly rod one more time, then decided to call it quits. She secured the line, and waited until she caught her husband's attention. He was fishing farther downstream. When he looked her way, she waved then turned to point to the shore to show him she was through for the day. That's when she saw the grizzly bear on the bank of the stream. It was sitting, much like a human might do. Her nine year old daughter was propped on one massive leg and pulling at the fur on the bear's huge front paws. She was laughing.

"Oh my God! Ron!" Elaine screamed. "Come quick! Ronnnalllldd! Hurry!"

Nine year old Samantha Douglas hung on to huge bear and glanced toward the stream at the sound of her mother's voice. She laughed and stood up on the bear's back leg and wrapped her arms around a front one. "Look, Mom!" she shouted gleefully as the bear slowly raised its front leg and lifted her into the air, then set her back down as carefully as a mother placing a baby in its cradle.

Elaine Douglas looked on in horror. Her throat constricted, leaving her unable to utter another word. At the same time Ronald Douglas saw what was happening.

"Sammie! Get away from that bear!" His voice came out high and shrill, fraught with fear. He dropped his fly rod and began splashing towards the shore, his progress impeded by the heavy waders and thigh-deep water. As he ran, he fumbled for a grasp on the .38 caliber revolver holstered at his chest. He struggled toward his daughter while his thoughts skittered wildly, wondering what effect his pistol would have on a half-ton bear and whether he would have time to find out before the grizzly killed his daughter.

"Sammie, get away!" he screamed again. He was scared to death that any moment the bear would hug Samantha to its chest and mangle her as easily as him wadding up a piece of scrap paper.

Samantha was an obedient child. She looked up at the bear's huge head, with its mouth open and tongue lolling. It looked funny with one normal ear and one shortened and notched from an encounter with a bad tempered wolverine. Whoofluff had told her it happened when he was a cub. She spoke some words to the beast's good ear, then jumped off its leg. The bear made a deep snuffling noise at her as it got to its feet and ambled away. It had a peculiar gait to its walk from two missing toes on a back paw, courtesy of the same wolverine that had mangled its ear. A moment later Samantha was almost being crushed in the embrace of both her parents.

"Sammie, don't you *ever* go near a bear again," Mrs. Douglas admonished once she could speak coherently again.

"But Mom, he wasn't going to hurt me. He said he'd be careful."

"Oh Lord, not that again," Mr. Douglas said. His hands were still trembling, but the bear was already out of sight and he could feel his pulse slowing down. He noticed that he was still holding his pistol and quickly re-holstered it. "Sammie, animals can't talk. I've told you that over and over. Why don't you listen to me?"

"I know Daddy, but they *think* like they're talking. Whoofluff just wanted to play with me. He said so."

"Whoofluff?"

"That's his name. He said he'll be back again sometime soon. He likes to play with me."

"Well, you're not to play with him again, do you understand!" Mrs. Douglas almost screamed at her daughter, horrified at what might have happened. In Alaska there were numerous stories of humans being killed and eaten by the big grizzlies.

"But Mom, he..."

"I don't want to hear it! It was bad enough when you brought that pair of raccoons home. Wild animals are dangerous, Samantha! Don't you understand that?"

Samantha hung her head and didn't answer. She didn't know *how* to answer. No one believed her when she told them animals talked. And the bears wouldn't hurt her, not the ones she played with, like Whoofluff, or Loosmuff and her cubs, Soomum and Kolpumf, which Mom and Dad hadn't seen her with.

"Do you understand, young lady?!" Mrs. Douglas gripped Samantha by her upper arms. She was so emotionally wrought that she couldn't decide whether to shake her daughter's teeth loose or hug her to death.

"Yes'm," Samantha said. Neither parent noticed she had one hand behind her back, fingers crossed.

Whoofluff was disappointed when the little human cub wasn't by the stream the next time he stopped to drink. He had encountered a few humans before, but she was the only one he knew who could talk to him and wasn't afraid to come near. She was one of his few interests in life besides food and drink and female bears at the proper time. He decided to see if he could find her again. He snuffled around the ground by the stream where she and the grown humans had been until he found their scent. He followed it slowly until he was sure of the direction, then speeded up, heading toward the place where he knew the human herd lived.

Saturday was the day when the families of the little village of Wikluk normally did their weekly shopping at the combination general store and post office. It was located on the unpaved road named Main Street, which in fact was the only street in the village. The Douglas family were just carrying their last bundles out to their car when the shouts began.

"Good God, it's a bear!"

"Quick! Somebody bring a gun!"

Samantha stopped abruptly. She cocked her head like an alert bird listening for worms, then dropped her package of groceries and began running pell mell down the street. She didn't have far to go since there were only two other commercial buildings and a couple of dozen houses in Wikluk.

"Sammie, come back!" Mr. Douglas called desperately, already knowing what his daughter must be up to. He discarded his bags and took off after her, followed by Mrs. Douglas, who had an agonized look on her face to match that of her husband. Samantha paid not the least bit of attention to their shouts, not after she heard mention of a gun. She whizzed down the street and disappeared around the corner of the last house on the street. She outdistanced Jeff Wesley, who was just coming outside with a rifle in his hands. The scruffy looking man always had a weapon handy.

Wesley, The Douglas couple and several other residents followed in Samantha's wake, spurred on by the sounds of horrendous screams coming from behind the house. As the band of townspeople ran past the yard and veered to the right, they all stopped abruptly, almost causing a pileup. The screams were coming from a young woman who had been out gardening. They cut off abruptly as she caught sight of the people following Samantha, then resumed even more shrilly as she saw the Douglas girl run full tilt, right into the bear.

Whoofluff ignored the hubbub and pretended the impact of Samantha hitting his bulk was sufficient to knock him over, even though he had barely felt the thump of her nine year old body. Samantha immediately jumped onto his amply padded belly, swollen from summer feeding. She laughed, then rolled off. She ran around in front of him and put her arms around his neck as he turned onto his side and raised his head. Whoofluff was so big they would barely reach. She hugged him and faced the crowd.

"Sammie! Move out of the way so he can shoot!" Mr. Douglas shouted at his daughter.

"No! He just wants to play! Don't shoot, Mr. Wesley! He won't hurt anybody!" The big bear got to its feet, causing Samantha to lose her hold on its neck, but she stood in front of it and spread her arms wide in a protective gesture. "Please don't shoot!"

The very idea of the small girl trying to protect a huge grizzly bear with her body was so incongruous that Mr. Wesley lowered the barrel of his weapon, even though he would have loved to kill the bear. Seeing Mr. Douglas beside him, he said, "What about it Ron? Should I risk a shot?"

"No. I think she'll be all right. She..." he hesitated for a moment, not wanting to admit publicly that his daughter thought bears could talk. "She sort of has a way with animals. Sammie!"

"Dad, it's *okay*. Whoofluff was just lonely and wanted to come play with me."

"Well, tell him to go away before someone shoots him."

"Yes, sir," Samantha said. She reached way up to hug the bear's neck while he lowered it to accommodate her.

Gasps came from the watching throng as she ruffled its thick fur. By then the ones watching the scene included almost every person who lived in Wikluk as well as the Saturday shoppers from the outback. Samantha tugged at Whoofluff's good ear and began talking to him. She spoke so softly that her words were indecipherable to anyone else. Mr. Douglas began edging closer, intending to snatch Samantha away if he got a chance. Jeff Wesley began circling around in order to get a clear shot. *The hell with Douglas*, he thought.

Samantha saw them coming closer and spoke louder. "Dad, can we buy Mrs. Mobley's strawberries? He really just came to play with me, but he got distracted by their smell. Please?"

Mr. Douglas looked toward the garden and saw an overturned straw basket. Samantha didn't seem to be in quite as much danger as he had thought, but it was still bad enough. *Anything to get that bear away from her!*

"Yes, yes, Sammie! I'll buy the strawberries. Now for goodness sake, see if you can get him to go away!"

"I will, but please, Dad, make everyone promise not to shoot him. He won't hurt anyone if they leave him alone."

Mr. Douglas hesitated.

"Please, Dad?" she pleaded. "I couldn't stand it if someone hurt Whoofluff." Just the thought caused a tear to escape and trickle down her face, weaving a streaked path. No fair maid on the ramparts of a castle crying for a knight to save her from the evil baron could have made a more appealing plea for help. Mr. Douglas turned around to face his friends and neighbors.

"Sammie says the bear will leave, but she wants everyone to promise not to harm him. Is that okay?"

A subdued muttering greeted his entreaty, but despite some dour faces, they all agreed not to hurt the bear if it would leave.

Jeff Wesley looked disgusted, but he nodded. *Damn bear, coming right into town, threatening people. I see him again I'll take care of that problem right quick, no matter what that silly little Douglas girl thinks!*

"Do they promise? They have to promise," Samantha said. She rubbed her face in Whoofluff's fur to wipe away the tears then looked back at the crowd.

Red-faced, and wondering what his friends and neighbors were thinking, Mr. Douglas relayed the request.

This time he heard a few nervous chuckles, but nods of heads and spoken answers indicated everyone agreed.

Promises to a bear! Next thing you know she'll be wanting us to stop catching salmon, Wesley thought, clutching his rifle. *Damn foolishness is what it is.*

"They all promise."

Samantha's face broke into a wide happy grin. She tugged affectionately at Whoofluff's pelt and said a few words to him, again too low to be heard.

The bear gobbled the remaining strawberries then walked away, not getting in a hurry but still covering the ground at a remarkably fast pace.

Mr. and Mrs. Douglas rushed forward and claimed their daughter.

All the time during the drive home, Samantha was unnaturally silent, where normally she was a chatterbox. For the first time since she discovered that animals could talk to her with their silent, abbreviated thoughts she was wondering why no one else could understand them. The problem was absorbing all her attention.

Once back home, Mrs. Douglas took her daughter aside for a heart to heart talk, an encounter she had been unconsciously avoiding, hoping Samantha would grow out of her imaginary conversations with animals.

"Sammie, what has gotten into you with this animal business? You have to stop it, do you hear? You know good and well that animals can't talk. It's time for you to drop this nonsense and begin growing up. You're not going to be a little girl much longer. You'll be a young lady. Ladies do not go around imagining they can talk to animals. "

"But Mom..."

"No, I don't want to hear excuses or stories about how animals talk to you. It's time to put that nonsense aside. Besides, didn't you see how frightened your father and I were?"

"You didn't have to be scared, Mom. Whoofluff just wanted to play. Honest."

"I don't care if he wanted to dance a jig with you. Either you put a stop to fraternizing with animals or I'm going to take away your library card. Is that clear?"

Fraternizing. That meant hanging around with. Samantha couldn't bear the thought of not being able to borrow books from the general store's library to read, especially when the satellite was sometimes down for a week at a time. She sighed. *Grownups just don't understand*, she thought. Aloud, she said "Yes, ma'am. I won't play with Woofluff any more." She held her breath, hoping her mother wouldn't notice she wasn't promising not to *talk* to Whoofluff. That wasn't playing.

"All right then, that's the end of it. Now let's get the groceries put away and you can help me make us a pie for dinner."

Jeff Wesley spent a lot of time in the forest. He didn't pay much attention to the game laws. When he needed meat for his family he took it. If an animal showed the least sign of threatening behavior, he shot it. Sometimes it didn't even have to be threatening him. He liked to kill animals. It gave him a feeling of superiority, of power.

Several days after Whoofluff appeared in town, Wesley was just completing the dressing of a young caribou that had become separated from its herd. It had wandered too close to his little house located on the road leading to Wikluk and naturally he had killed it. He was in a hurry to finish the job and get his meat inside and in the freezer. He didn't want to be caught with a caribou after the season was closed in the area. At the same time, Whoofluff was headed in the general direction of Wikluk. He was driven by a vague yearning to see the little human cub again when he crossed the path of Jeff Wesley. He sniffed, scenting the smell of fresh blood. Bears are never adverse to a bite to eat during the summer. A tremendous amount of food was necessary to store up fat to sustain them while they hibernated during the extreme cold of northern Alaska. As he got closer to the blood smell, another odor told him that one of the humans from the herd the girl cub belonged to was present.

Whoofluff's memory was directed almost exclusively toward food and drink and where and how to find it, but his mind had made room for the human cub who could talk to him. He also retained a few other odd bits of lore about humans.

Ordinarily Whoofluff was wary of the species. One of his other morsels of knowledge was the memory of seeing how easily humans could take the life force from animals. They did it by making loud noises from the odd smelling sticks some of them carried. But the girl cub had told him no one from her herd would hurt him. And she had quieted the hubbub over him eating some of the tasty berries the last time he saw her. Maybe this male human would be willing to share some of its kill, too. Confidently, sure that he would come to no harm, he waddled through the underbrush toward the man.

Wesley smelled the bear at the same time he heard it—and it was very near. His rifle was leaning against a tree several yards away. He cursed under his breath for being so careless, but Wesley never went anywhere without his pistol too, just to be on the safe side. He drew it from its holster and scanned the nearby brush. His eyes widened as he saw the bear, only a few short steps away. It was much nearer than he had thought. Then he noticed the scarred notched ear. *It's the same damned bear that crazy little Douglas brat kept me from killing in town!*

Whoofluff rumbled a greeting to the human and came closer. Wesley would have been fine if he had ignored the bear and simply left the caribou for him, but giving his kill to a bear was simply unthinkable. Besides, he purposely interpreted Whoofluff's deep-throated greeting as a threat so he would have an excuse to shoot despite that silly promise to the stupid Douglas girl.

Wesley was a knowledgeable woodsman and ordinarily wouldn't have dreamed of trying to kill a grizzly with a pistol, but this one was so close he couldn't miss, and the heavy .45 with the high powered loads made him overconfident. Remembering how he had been thwarted before, he raised his gun, aiming for the head.

Just as he fired, the bear dipped his head to sniff at some of the caribou offal he had discarded. The bullet plowed a furrow across the pelt and underlying fat of Whoofluff's shoulder. Startled and hurt, Whoofluff roared into action and reared up, faster than Wesley imagined possible. He slapped the gun away with one huge paw just as Wesley fired a second shot, causing him to miss completely. The blow flung the weapon into the brush.

Wesley screamed and ran for his rifle, but he got no farther than a couple of steps before Whoofluff was on him.

The Douglas family lived a couple of miles from Wikluk. It was nearing noon and Mr. Douglas and his daughter were outside, waiting on the mail jeep. When it arrived, the driver honked.

"Must be that book your mother ordered," Mr. Douglas said, then had second thoughts when the honking became urgent and the jeep turned into their driveway. He and Samantha met it at the front gate where the driveway stopped.

"Ron, you better get Samantha inside, then come on into town. Bring your rifle."

"Why? What's happened?"

"Jeff Wesley was found near his home. He was mauled to death by a bear."

"Good God! I didn't particularly like the man, but I hate to hear about anyone dying like that."

"Yeah. Well, just wanted to let you know. We'll get a hunt organized and take care of the brute before it gets a kid out berry picking or something."

"I'll get my rifle," Mr. Douglas said. "Samantha, get in the house and stay there until your mother gets home. Hear me?"

"Yes, sir."

The mailman waited until Mr. Douglas's daughter was walking away from them, then beckoned Douglas closer.

"I didn't want her to overhear, Ron, but judging from the footprints around the body, it was the same bear she made friends with in town. Thought you might want to know." He said nothing about the remains of the caribou at the site.

"Thanks, George. I appreciate it. I'll see you in town, soon as I fetch Elaine and send her home to watch Sammie."

As soon as Mr. Douglas was out of sight, Samantha left the house and raced into the woods, taking a short cut toward where Mr. Wesley lived. All the way, she was hoping desperately it wasn't one of the grizzlies she had made friends with, but she suspected it was. She remembered the disgusted look on Mr. Wesley's face when she made everyone promise not to hurt Whoofluff.

She arrived before the hunting party had even gotten organized. The body was gone, of course, but it was easy to tell where it had happened. The little scavengers were already busy with parts of the caribou carcass that had been left lying. In the distance she heard the howl of a wolf, but she barely noticed. All her attention was concentrated on examining the area for bear footprints.

"Oh no," Samantha said to herself when she saw the distinctive impression, a paw print with two toes missing. "*Whoofluff. It was Whoofluff!* She began following the tracks, then as soon as she was certain of the direction, she began running through the woods again. A while later she arrived at the stream where Mom and Dad had seen her playing with the big grizzly. She was panting from the long run.

"Whoofluff!" she called. "Whoofluff, it's me. Come out!"

There was a rustling in the brush and the bear walked up to her. It lowered its head so she could get her arms around its huge neck. It was then that she saw the streak of dried blood running down from his shoulder.

"You're hurt! Poor Whoofluff. How did it happen?"

The bear told her how he had ran across Mr. Wesley while he was cutting up the caribou. Recognizing him as one of the human herd the girl cub had said wouldn't hurt him, he uttered a greeting and came nearer, hoping the man would share some of his kill. Despite his politeness, the man inflicted a painful wound with the little stick that made a loud noise anyway, and was going to hurt him some more with the big stick if he could. That was when Whoofluff became angry and knocked him to the ground and bit him. Hard.

"That mean old man, and after he promised, too!" Samantha said to Whoofluff. "It serves him right, but now you have to go away. Go 'way off, Whoofluff, or the men will hunt you down and kill you. Please?"

The huge grizzly bear nuzzled his little human friend and turned away. Bears can't cry, but if they could, Whoofluff would have shed some tears at the thought of never seeing the little girl cub again, the only human he knew who could talk to bears.

As she watched him go, Samantha did cry. She let the tears flow freely as she trudged back home, no longer hurrying.

Samantha heard Mom and Dad frantically calling her name and speeded up a little. If Dad was already back home she must have been gone longer than she thought.

"Sammie! Oh God, where have you been? Didn't I tell you to stay inside?" Mr. Douglas was almost overwhelmed with relief at finding his daughter safe and sound. He had been frightened out of his wits when he returned from town and found her missing.

Mrs. Douglas was so distraught she couldn't even talk. She simply hugged her daughter close and whimpered.

Eventually, the three were back in the house, and by this time Samantha's parents were demanding an explanation for her absence.

"I had to go warn Whoofluff so he wouldn't get shot," Samantha said, knowing the adults would be furious, but she wanted to explain.

"Do you mean to tell me you went and saw that ... that man-eating bear after you said you wouldn't play with him again?" her mother asked, horrified at the thought.

"I wasn't playing with him. I was just *talking* to him, Mom. I told him to go way away from here so he wouldn't get shot."

"Well, he needs to be shot for killing and eating poor Mr. Wesley."

"Oh, Mom! He didn't eat anybody. He didn't even mean to kill Mr. Wesley. He just wanted to keep from being hurt any more. Mr. Wesley *shot* him, after he *promised*. People shouldn't break promises."

"Lord have mercy," Mrs. Douglas said, looking to the heavens. "Ronald, what are we going to do with her?"

"Put her in a circus if this goes on," Mr. Douglas answered aloud. *My God, I think she really can talk to animals* he said to himself, very silently.

"Be serious, Ronald! She could have been killed!"

"Whoofluff wouldn't hurt me, Mom, any more than Loosmuff or her cubs would."

As soon as she saw Mr. and Mrs. Douglas exchange startled glances, Samantha knew she had made a mistake.

"And just who might Loosmuff be, young lady? Another bear, I presume?"

Samantha hung her head. "Yes'm, a mother bear," she murmured, her voice barely audible.

"Did I hear you say '*cubs*'," Mr. Douglas asked, aghast at the thought of his daughter going anywhere near a mother bear with cubs. They were notorious for the aggressiveness with which they defended their progeny. *If she can get away with that, then she really must be able to talk to animals. Bears, anyway. Good Lord.*

"Loosmuff didn't mind, Dad. She knew I wouldn't hurt them."

She wouldn't hurt them? *How about the bear hurting* her? *Obviously, the mother bear had been as friendly to her as the one in town. Amazing.* Mr. Douglas nodded, finally convinced.

But Mrs. Douglas was still angry. "You're never to go near a bear again!" she shouted at Samantha, fearful of her only child's safety making her voice sound furious.

Samantha was momentarily saved from further recriminations by the sound of honking outside. Two jeeps with armed men in them had stopped by to pick up Mr. Douglas. They were on their way toward Wesley's place to begin the hunt.

Mr. Douglas started toward the door, then hesitated. He turned back around. "Sammie, which direction did you tell the bear to go?"

She looked up at her father, a despondent expression on her face. Then her eyes widened. She started to smile as she saw the slow, careful wink Mr. Douglas gave her, out of sight of her mother's unsympathetic gaze. She raised her arm and pointed in the opposite direction that Whoofluff had taken. "That way, Dad."

"I'll be back later," he said.

The hunters never did find Whoofluff, and the bear never returned to the vicinity of Wikluk again.

CHAPTER TWO

It was several weeks before Mrs. Douglas would let Samantha out of her sight, but eventually she relaxed. As Summer neared its end, the Douglas household was almost back to normal. So normal, in fact, that Mrs. Douglas agreed to host Samantha's tenth birthday party at their home.

Wikluk and the area around it was so sparsely populated that there wouldn't be many children attending, but nevertheless, Samantha was looking forward to it eagerly. She would be starting fifth grade in another month.

The day dawned beautifully. An early cool front chased the mosquito swarms away. Mrs. Douglas made a large beautiful Salmon Berry cake with white icing and somehow managed to find a package of candles in the general store. The cake was graced with eleven candles. Ten for her birthday and one to grow on.

A dozen of her friends were supposed to be there, some coming from miles away, with their parents making special trips to bring them to the party. Mr. Douglas had made certain that his duties with the Alaskan Environmental Assessment office allowed him to be present as well. Sometimes his duties kept him away from home for weeks on end.

The home of Ronald and Elaine Douglas was fairly typical of rural Alaska. It was snug, well insulated and built to withstand the tree-bursting cold of winters in the northern part of the state. It had been built on a knoll higher than the surrounding area, allowing an adequate path for drainage of the spring snow-melt into a small creek a hundred yards below. The yard and garden were cleared, as well as the drive leading up to the gravel road that serviced the little town of Wikluk. Beyond that forest predominated, broken only by game trails and isolated meadows.

Wildlife was abundant in the area. Grizzly bears fed on salmon where the creek fed into a slightly larger stream, the spawning bed of the delicious fish after their long and tortuous journey from the ocean. Caribou and elk roamed the forest as well as smaller varieties of ruminants, all of which provided prey for wolves, mountain lions, black bears and grizzlies. It was usually the old and weak and the very young which fell to the teeth and claws of the carnivores. When opportunity presented smaller predators like wolverines and bobcats and lynx sometimes managed to kill the larger animals but mostly they stuck to rabbits, partridge and the like. Other animals were present as well. Beaver, fox, weasel, voles, and a plethora of others all played their part in the intricate dance of life, reproduction and death.

Samantha could communicate with most of them, although the more intelligent the animal, the plainer their thoughts. Frequently, on her way to and from Wikluk when the weather was nice and she could walk she had trysts with some of her favorites, like Brfcut the old bull moose who hung out by the lake above the little stream and Hostervut, the alpha male wolf which led the pack that roamed the area around the village.

Hostervut was fun to talk to. He was young to be an alpha male but his strength and cunning earned him the position. He was also a big beautiful animal. He sported a thick dark brown pelt with a black-tipped, bushy tail. Hostervut had just reached his full body weight, almost a hundred pounds, large for a timber wolf. Consequently, he had very little competition from other males or females for the leadership position.

Game had been extra plentiful the year of Samantha's tenth birthday. The pack was well fed, leaving ample time for Hostervut and others of the pack to turn their attention to matters besides food. Since none of the females were in heat, that left time for those of the pack who had such a notion to indulge in play and curiosity. The cubs, those less than a year old, were particularly prone to play when they were well fed. Whenever Samantha had an opportunity, she sneaked into the woods and rubbed old Brfcut's antlers where they itched from the last growth or found Hostervut and asked his permission to play with the cubs. The alpha wolf was glad to grant it and the mothers of the cubs didn't mind a bit once Samantha assured them she would baby sit while they took the opportunity to grab a nap. Her favorites were the youngest cubs, Betus, Cetus and Ketus. They loved to act fierce and tug at the strange fur the human cub covered herself with, or roll in the grass with her while she rubbed their tummies and listened to their puppy growls of pleasure.

The culmination of Samantha's birthday party was intended to be a demonstration of magic, performed by an itinerant showman who flew his own plane over a wide area.

Ronald and Elaine Douglas were proud of themselves for thinking of this way to let Samantha know they were pleased with her. So was no longer making a spectacle of herself by claiming she could talk to animals. Not once in the last several months had they seen her with any animal other than the barn cat who earned his keep as a mouser. The only exception was Brfcut, the old moose, who was so gentle they allowed her to feed it and keep it on the place year round as a sort of free-roaming pet. Even then, it had taken a number of demonstrations before Mrs. Douglas relented, and only because her husband had suggested that letting her talk to a harmless old moose would keep her away from bears and wolverines.

Elaine Douglas didn't believe for a minute the old bull moose understood a thing Samantha said to him, but it had been a fair compromise. She also never saw the winks that passed between her husband and her daughter. Mr. Douglas believed Samantha could really make at least a few animals understand what she said, although he still cautioned her about going near carnivores like bears. But even he didn't believe animals could really talk to her or she to them, not in any meaningful way.

Samantha laughed gaily after she blew all eleven candles out with one huge breath. The few adults and all the children cheered and clapped at her achievement, then Mrs. Douglas began serving the cake and ice cream outside on Mr. Douglas' homemade picnic benches. They were made of logs split in half lengthwise and propped on cross sections of other logs. However, Samantha couldn't help but notice her parents both kept stealing glances toward where the airfield lay, the only means of egress in and out of the village.

Bush pilots served most of Alaska. The state was so huge and so wild and untamed that roads were scarce and in most areas small light planes were the only means of transporting people and cargo. She knew the plane carrying Merlin Marston, the magician who was to perform at her party, was way overdue. It should have arrived that morning.

Once the cake and ice cream had been consumed with the alacrity that only tweens and teens can manage, Elaine Douglas motioned for Samantha to come inside the house with her. Heart dropping, Samantha followed her mother, knowing already what the summons meant.

"Sammie, we're so sorry," Mrs. Douglas began once Samantha was seated, "but ... well..." She hesitated, not really wanting to break the bad news.

"But Mr. Marston isn't coming."

"I'm sorry, baby, but there was an accident. His plane lost a motor as he was taking off, and he had to return."

"Can't it be fixed?" Samantha asked hopefully.

"No, not today. It needs a part that's not in stock and you know it's too dangerous to fly with only one engine."

Samantha knew. Children grew up in Alaska with bush pilots as much their heroes as movie stars or rock musicians.

"What will we do, then?"

Elaine Douglas had been thinking of that very predicament. "Your father suggested you take the kids and show them around the place. Hardly any of them have been here before and he thought they might like to see the shop. After that you can take them two by two to the waterfall on the Mule and let them see the rainbows and watch you scratch the moose's antlers."

Samantha could hardly believe her ears. Her father was going to let her drive her friends on the Mule, a refurbished World War II flat bed light supply hauler that was his pride and joy. Not only that, her mother was actually going to let her talk to Brfcut while others were present! She knew her mother didn't believe she and Brfcut understood each other, but who cared? They knew and maybe some of her friends and classmates would believe her once she showed them. It was almost as good as having the magic show!

Mr. Douglas had welded safety rails and bars in the cargo space of the Mule and attached an old car seat behind the driver's space for two passengers to ride on. When the groans and grumbles and tears over the announcement that the magician had plane trouble and couldn't make it subsided, Mr. Douglas grinned. "But!" he said, "We have another surprise for you! Sammie is going to give you all a ride on our Mule, two at a time, to our waterfall and..." He had to stop and explain to shouts and questions that the Mule was not an animal but a rare and expensive vehicle, a collector's item that very few kids ever got to ride on and that Samantha would be driving them, "...and then, once you get to our waterfall, we have two treats for you. The first is letting you see how sunlight and mist can create beautiful natural spectacles such as rainbows, but the second is even better. Can you guess what it is?"

Of course none of the children could guess; he had simply paused for dramatic effect.

"All right, since you can't guess, I'll tell you. Sammie is going to show you one of her special friends, a bull moose! Up close!" He paused again to let them digest this information and then gave them the kicker. "And even better, Sammie will show you how to do something very few people have ever done in their life. She'll ask her friend the moose to let you scratch his antlers! They are shedding their velvet now and are very sensitive and they itch. The moose will be very grateful for you scratching him where he itches! How about that?"

Yells and cries of enthusiasm greeted the end of his announcement, tempered only by the doubtful looks of the few other adults present.

"Ron..." One of the mothers began, but he smiled and held up his hand to stop her. "Don't worry, Judy. This is a tame old Moose and you know Sammie has a ... well, a way with animals. It's perfectly safe. She's kept the old fellow for a pet for the last year since the young bulls pushed him out of the herd. He just loves to have Sammie scratch his antlers. You know how they itch his time of year."

"Well ... okay, if you say it's safe. The kids were really disappointed when Merlin's plane broke down."

"It's perfectly safe, I promise."

Mr. Douglas called Samantha to the side before allowing her to begin transporting her guests. "Now Sammie, I want you to drive careful. Each time you get two passengers to the waterfall, tell them to stay close to the cabin, just in case a grizzly happens by. And until they're all there make certain that your moose stays on the other side of the stream, just to be sure. Okay?"

"Well ... okay, Dad. He wouldn't hurt anyone but I'll tell him to stay on the other side until we're ready. I guess he can wait that long to get his antlers scratched."

"That's the way I want it for today."

Samantha smiled. "Then that's how we'll do it. They'll probably like it better that way anyhow. I guess old Brfcut could seem kinda scary if you can't talk to him like I can."

Douglas nodded, wondering once again just how much Samantha could really understand of an animal's thoughts. Some days he believed her utterly when she said she could talk to creatures of the wild, but in bright daylight his young daughter seemed perfectly normal and he believed hardly any of what she told him.

"Where's your moose?" Jed, a burly boy who was somewhat of a bully asked as he jumped from the Mule. He and another boy were the last two members of the party Samantha had brought to the waterfall.

"Just look at the rainbows for now," she replied. "Aren't they pretty?

"They're beautiful," Sinuteit, a girl with an Inuit mother and Italian father agreed. "And there's lots of them if you stand just right."

"I want to see the moose," Jed insisted. "You said he'd be here."

"Yeah," his friend said. "Who wants to stare at rainbows all day?"

Samantha didn't answer at once. She didn't particularly like Jed or Bradley, either. They were the two oldest boys in the little school that handled children up through the seventh grade. They would be moving on next year if they managed to graduate, which thought was doubtful. She wouldn't have invited them to her party had her parents not insisted, but since they were here, she supposed finding the big ungulate and showing him off was in order. Except ... she glanced at the ground and saw prints, but they hadn't been made by hooves. They were paw prints, big ones.

Oh, drat! She thought. *Hostervut has been nosing around here and scared Brfcut off! He doesn't like wolves, even after I asked Hostervut not to hurt him. Now what do I do?*

"I bet she didn't have a moose here at all," Samantha heard one of the boys say. It made her mad, but she had no idea how to answer the charge—until she heard a rustle of underbrush, barely audible over the increasingly frustrated noises coming from her classmates. She looked in that direction and saw a black nose and two eyes, shining in the darkened brushy alcove from reflected sunlight. A wolf was watching her!

She hurried over to the heavy growth and parted it with her hands. A full grown female wolf looked back at her. "Tetmulic! What are you doing here? Where are your pups?" she said.

Hunting has been poor since the caribou left. I came here hoping to find you and beg some food. The wolf's words weren't that articulate, of course, but Samantha understood her perfectly. She thought for a moment, then smiled as an idea came to her.

"If they feed your pups, would you let the human cubs play with them?" Samantha asked the mother wolf.

Any animal Samantha talked to always trusted her. After all, she was the only human they knew who could speak to the animals of the forest.

Yes she agreed. *You must help me care for them, though.*

"Of course!" she agreed immediately. She ran to tell the other kids.

"Now they're not used to humans, so you have to be very careful with them," Samantha warned. "Don't try to force the pups to do anything they don't want to or *Tetmulic* will take them back into the forest. Just hold out bits of food and let them take it from your hands."

"Who's Tetmulic?"

"That's the mother wolf. Right there!" She pointed dramatically as the big animal came out of the brush, trailed by four fuzzy, bumbling pups five or six weeks old. A few minutes later, all the kids had completely forgotten about a moose and were vying with each other to feed the scraps of their meal to the wolf pups. Once the last bit of food was gone, Samantha had them sit in a circle with Tetmulic and her pups in the center. The pups were ready to play now, and they did, with their mother watching benignly. It went so well that time flew and before Samantha quite knew what was happening, her father strode into the clearing by the waterfall and cabin.

Mr. Douglas was wise enough to realize what was going on, but he was frightened. What if that mother wolf with the pups became agitated at his appearance? She might do anything, thinking she had to protect her progeny.

"Sammie," he said quietly. "It's time to go."

"Oh, I'm sorry, Dad. I wasn't watching the time. Okay, everyone can pet Tetmulic one time to thank her for letting you play with her puppies, then we have to go."

Mr. Douglas held his breath as one by one the children stroked the full grown timber wolf. It outweighed half of them and could have torn the throat from any of them in a second had it been so inclined. But after it had been petted by each child, the circle broke and the mother wolf made a gruff noise, telling her pups it was time to go.

"Would you like to pet her, Dad? Her name is Tetmulic. She would like it, I think. She knows you're my father and we gave a lot of our food to her pups."

The wolf strode quickly to the elder Douglas, but rather than stand to be petted, she raised her forequarters and put her front paws on his chest. Dazed, he began scratching behind her ears and on the top of her head, wondering if anyone would believe him if he told this story. On the other hand, he suddenly decided not to say anything. The children's parents probably wouldn't be so sanguine about them playing with wolf pups and their mother as he was!

Mr. Douglas thought Samantha could only communicate with selected animals. Mrs. Douglas didn't believe even that much. She thought her daughter just had a way with animals. Unknown to the elder Douglases, Samantha could communicate with almost any mammal although she was very careful not to let her parents know how often and how varied were her trysts with them. Perhaps she wouldn't have gone into the forest so often had Mrs. Douglas allowed her to have a pet, but she was adamantly against it, since pets had to live inside homes during the fierce Alaskan winters.

Despite her father warning Samantha to keep quiet about what happened at the culmination of her birthday party and her asking the guests not to tell their parents, the story got out. As it made the rounds at school and among the townspeople of Wikluk, it became greatly exaggerated until the tale had Samantha leading a whole pack of wolves to the birthday party and subjecting everyone there to fear of being torn apart.

Religious individuals began whispering about witches and deals with the Devil. The school children and teachers alike began ostracizing her. It became such a problem that one day she came home from school early, in tears.

Mrs. Douglas hugged her and tried to allay the hurt by treating it as a "passing incident".

"I told you to quit pretending you can talk to animals, didn't I?" she asked.

"But Mom, I can talk to them! I can, I can, I can!"

Mr. Douglas entered the room at that moment. He quickly analyzed the situation, but had no time to stake out a position before his wife jumped all over him.

"Ronald, this has gone far enough. No, it's gone way too far. You simply have to put a stop to it, right this moment."

He looked helplessly toward Samantha and shrugged his shoulders. He knew there was no way he could convince his wife Samantha actually did have such a talent. Mrs. Douglas didn't want to have a daughter who was that abnormal and she had closed her mind to the very possibility that she could talk to animals.

"Dad, you know I can, don't you? The animals don't really talk, but they *think* like they're talking and I can hear it just like it was a voice. Mom, how do you think I got Tetmulic to let us play with her puppies?"

"And I suppose Tet ... tetlu whatever is the wolf's name?" Mrs. Douglas said. Her voice dripped with sarcasm.

"Elaine, she can communicate with animals. You know she can."

The woman set her face firmly in its "no nonsense" expression. "She cannot talk to animals, Ronald. The most she is capable of is perhaps showing no fear so they don't attack her. But she has to get out of that or one day one of those dangerous creatures will wind up hurting her."

"Mom, I don't play with animals that are dangerous. Besides, I could tell if they were. And they *like* me. They think it's wonderful that at least one person can talk to them when no one else can."

Her mother threw up her hands in defeat and trounced from the room. But Samantha and her father knew they hadn't heard the last of it.

Samantha endured the school days by anticipating the three o'clock bell when she could go home and talk with the chipmunk and little half grown rabbit while pretending to help in the garden. Both animals lived at the edge of the fence and had created tunnels to get into the rows of lettuce, carrots, and other vegetable they liked. However, talking to them was rather like conversing with a not too bright baby just learning to say da-da and ma-ma. Most of their thoughts were of food, avoiding the weasel that periodically came into the area seeking prey, and curiosity about the human cub who could miraculously speak their language, such as it was.

Samantha never interfered with the food chain of the animals because she knew they accepted it as simply part of life. She also knew all animals thought of humans as the top predator in the endless cycle of life. It was disheartening many times but she realized animals had to eat, just as she did and she had learned to accept it.

After talking to the chipmunk named Buk and the rabbit named Per, she found herself longing for a brighter animal to converse with. There was no chance though, because Mrs. Douglas watched her very closely to make sure she didn't sneak off into the woods.

Curiously, it was an animal coming to Wikluk that capped the disparagement, scorn, and ridicule Samantha was being subjected to. Ordinarily, Alaska has little problem with rabies but any time a creature came down with the disease it was naturally a cause for great alarm. Anyone who was bitten would have to wait while the anti-viral serum was flown in, then take the excruciatingly painful shots for a period of ten days.

The wolverine was in the last stages of rabies when it wandered into the school grounds. Wolverines are bad tempered at best and really evil when stirred up, like this one was from its unquenchable thirst and constant pain.

Samantha heard the screams from the bench she was sitting on and having lunch with several other girls. She looked up and saw the animal approaching a group of first and second graders who were frozen by fear at the grunting, slavering, dirty and snarling wolverine, who wanted nothing so much as to have its sickness end. Animals have no concept of suicide however, or this one would certainly have done itself in somehow.

Samantha immediately ran toward the children and put herself between them and the wolverine.

Please don't bite any of them she pleaded. *Be nice and I'll help you end your pain and suffering.*

It snarled at her while ropes of saliva drooled from its open mouth, revealing very sharp white teeth. Samantha knew the saliva was loaded with the lethal infective stuff of rabies, but she stood fast.

I promise, she assured it again, while the madness roiled in its brain. *Just wait right here for a little while. Will you?*

It thought about its predicament for a moment then decided to let the human cub see what it could do. But only if it could stand the crazy, vile thoughts whirling in its mind for a little while longer without going into a raging storm or violence. It lay down on the grass in front of her. Samantha approached and stroked its head, talking to it soothingly. She could tell by its garbled speech that its mind was mostly gone. She hoped it could concentrate on staying put long enough for someone to return with a gun.

Time seemed to stretch out endlessly as she knelt by the crazed wolverine. The younger children waited, unable to get past her and the sick animal and into the confines of the school house. Each time one moved, the wolverine snarled and slavered. Samantha stroked it, telling it to please wait.

At last a nearby shop owner appeared with a rifle. "Stand Back, girl!" he yelled at her. The noise caused the rabid creature to move under Samantha's soothing hand.

Just a little longer. It will be over. I'm going to stand up and move. Shut your eyes and your suffering will end.

The madness abated a moment at the thought of the pain that made it crazy and sick would go away. It closed its eyes, waiting.

Samantha stood up and backed away, not wanting to get splattered with infective particles when it was shot. The sound of the rifle boomed through the schoolyard. The Wolverine shuddered, twitched, then rolled over and died.

"What were you thinking of you crazy girl?" The man who shot the rabid animal shouted. "You know it could have bitten you and given you rabies, too!"

"It wouldn't bite me. I told it to stay still and someone would put it out of its misery. It did."

She walked away, then went to the bathroom and washed her hands thoroughly. When she came out, teachers were waiting on her. They stared at her as if she were a goblin---or a witch. The other students looked at her as if she were crazy. Brave, but crazy just the same. All of them had heard of rabid animals and knew what they could do.

A few minutes later her mother arrived. She was concerned but it was covered by the grimness of her expression. After a brief explanation, she turned to her daughter. "Come on, we're going home."

That night Samantha was sent to bed early so that she couldn't hear the discussion taking place between her parents. Nothing was said the next day, nor the next. Or at least she heard nothing but snatches of conversation that were meaningless without knowing the whole context. When she went to school, she was avoided. There had been talk before but after the wolverine incident it grew ugly. Parents told their children to avoid her for fear she might infect them with her strange ideas. The third day afterward one teacher flatly refused to have her in her class. She was sent to the principal's office. The principal called Mrs. Douglas to come get her child.

Although she was told to sit outside the office while her mother talked to the principal there was no-one there to make her sit. It was nearing noon and the secretary had gone for lunch. Samantha stood near the closed door of the principal's office and she overheard what the school head said to her mother.

"I'm sorry, but you'll have to withdraw her from school. These people are just normal folks and they don't understand a child who can ... can ... well, they think she's a shaman or a witch. At the very least they think her idea of being able to talk to animals could spread and endanger their children. They fear they might try to talk to a bear or a wolf like she has and get hurt, or even killed. And frankly, Mrs. Douglas, people are beginning to say that if she is that abnormal then you must be, too."

There was more but Samantha buried her face in her hands then when that didn't work she put her hands over her ears. Now she did sit down, just as far from the closed door as she could get. She didn't want to hear anything else. Just because she understood animals, she, and now her mother were both thought to be demons of some sort. It was so terrible and so unfair.

The tear marks on her cheeks were still there as her mother came back outside. Elaine Douglas' face was white and strained but for the first time since the incident with the wolverine she spoke gently to her daughter.

"Come on, Sammie. Let's go home. We'll take care of this problem there."

"We're moving," Mr. Douglas announced the next morning at the breakfast table. "I've found a job at Angelina College in Texas where I can teach environmental issues. And Sammie ... when we go there, no matter what you can do with animals, you're not to let anyone know. You've seen what happens when people think you're different. We love you and I understand, but you'll just have to keep it a secret. Okay?"

"Okay, Dad. I will, I promise. But ... what if an animal *wants* to talk to me? I can't help it if I hear it and it wouldn't be nice not to answer."

"Oh, Lord," Mrs. Douglas declared. "I can't stand any more of this. Sammie..."

"Tell you what, Sammie," Mr. Douglas interjected, "When we get settled, we'll get you your own puppy to be a companion to you. Maybe even a kitten, too. How would that be?"

Samantha broke into a big smile for the first time in weeks. "Oh, that would be wonderful! But, Mom..."

"Your mother has agreed you can have a dog when we find a house."

"Oh thank you, Mom. Thank you!" She got up from the table and hugged her mother. She wondered why she had changed her mind about a pet in the house after all these years, but she wasn't going to argue.

"I promise I'll just try to talk to him alone!" she said.

Neither of her parents told her that allowing her to have a pet was a compromise they had reached, thinking perhaps it would keep her from seeking out animals. And moving to a small city instead of living near a forest would surely put a stop to her conversing with wild animals. Neither of them noticed she said she would only *try* not to talk to animals other than the dog, not that she would.

All in all, it seemed a happy solution for everyone.

CHAPTER THREE

Lufkin is a city of about 50,000 in the heart of East Texas. Angelina State College is located on the southern rim of the city. It is a small school but highly rated academically. Ronald Douglas found himself fitting in well there, teaching environmental science. Southwest of the city and near the campus he and Mrs. Douglas found a home they liked in a new subdivision outside city limits but not too close to any of the pine, oak and sweetgum forests of the area. They thought that would keep Samantha away from wild animals. That and her new companions.

First came Shafus, the German Shepherd puppy. She went with her parents to the home of the man who advertised the puppies for sale. Samantha was almost tempted to ask for the mother dog, but she knew it was a hopeless request. She squatted down near the animal.

"You're a good mother," she said to the big female dog as she nursed her pups.

The dog looked up at her with as curious an expression as possible for a dog. *You can talk. I wish my lady and man could do that.* To everyone but Samantha it simply sounded like a series of whoofs, whines and low friendly growls.

"I wish everyone could," Samantha told her. "May I take one of your puppies? I promise to give him a good home and love him just like you do."

I know you will. You talk to animals.

"Thank You," Samantha said. The dog wasn't talking in English sentences but she could understand her perfectly.

As she carried on the one-sided conversation with the mother dog in English just as if it could understand her, the dog's owner looked at her curiously then at Mr. and Mrs. Douglas.

Mrs. Douglas leaned close to him and whispered "She thinks she can talk to animals."

He nodded sadly. *A handicapped girl. And so pretty, too.*

"If you'll all go up front I'll take the pup you want. Bella would probably get angry if one of you touched them. Just as he said that he opened his mouth in horror.

Samantha had picked up one of the male pups and was cuddling it to her chest. She reached out and scratched Bella's ears and accepted a lick on her hand, then stood up. "I'll take this one. His name is Shafus."

"I don't believe it," Bella's owner declared as Samantha gave the big German Shepherd a last pat on the head and looked at her parents.

"We can go now. I told Bella that I'd take good care of Shafus for her."

"Sammie, I've told you to be more careful around animals and you just don't seem to want to listen," Mrs. Douglas said despairingly after they were away from the house and couldn't be overheard.

"Mom, I've told you and told you I can talk to animals. I would never go near one that would hurt me. I'd know. Not that I think any animal ever would."

Her mother rolled her eyes, hoping desperately that her daughter would confine her delusion to this one dog and the promised kitten.

"Why did you name the puppy Shafus?" Mr. Douglas asked once they were home.

"Oh, that was already his name. Bella told me. He knows it already." Samantha was sitting on the floor with the puppy in her lap.

"He does?"

"Sure. Call his name and watch."

"Shafus? Shafus!" he called.

The puppy turned around in her lap and looked in the direction from where the voice had come from.

"Hmm. Well, maybe he does but it could have just been the sound of my voice."

"You'll see," she said.

Mrs. Douglas was amazed at how quickly Shafus was housebroken, but not Samantha.

The first time he piddled in the floor, she petted him and said "Shafus, you can't do this indoors. Come on, let's go outside and I'll show you where to go in the future."

Errf? Shafus whimpered in his little puppy voice. He liked his new mistress. Unlike her mother's person, this one could *talk* to him, in language he could understand. He was so happy he wanted to do anything in the world to please her.

Shafus was brought home the first part of summer vacation so that he and Samantha spent much of their time together the first months of his new environment. He was very smart and had to be told only once not to stray from the yard or to chew up shoes. He never got into trouble over all the sins little puppies are usually prone to as they began exploring the world around them. Mrs. Douglas was so happy that he was a good and obedient dog that she bought Samantha a book about the history of dogs.

Samantha discovered that dogs had evolved over tens of thousands of years to be companions to humans. This was surprising, but not too much. She already knew that her new pet quickly grew to adore her in a way no other species of animal ever would or could. It was humbling to listen to the puppy burble his love in dog language, a love enhanced by her ability to converse with him. It became so deep and all encompassing to Shafus that she thought he would die if anything ever happened to her. And she knew without asking that Shafus would protect her to the death.

"He's a smart little fellow, isn't he, Elaine?" Mr. Douglas said one day.

"That's because he understands when I tell him something," Samantha said. "Isn't that it, Shafus?"

"*Woof!*" Shafus barked.

That was what the adult Douglas' heard. To Samantha, he agreed that he was a good dog because he could understand Samantha.

"Nonsense!" Mrs. Douglas exclaimed. "Honey, he's just a smart dog and he likes you. Oh, I'll admit you do have a way with animals but there is no way a dog can understand human language. Not like us."

"But he always understands me, Mom. All animals do. Of course none of them are as smart as Shafus. He's already learned to stay in the yard and when we go walking he looks both ways before we cross a street." As she spoke she thought the words to her puppy. She had gradually come to understand that was how animals understood her and it wasn't usually necessary for her to speak out loud at all although it was helpful when she wanted to make her wishes known in detail.

Mrs. Douglas shook her head and looked at her husband. He shrugged, not wanting to get into the old argument again. Mrs. Douglas left the room.

"Honey, you aren't going to convince your mother," he said to Samantha. "It would be best if you just don't say things like that to her. Okay?"

"Uh-huh," she nodded. "But, Dad, you believe me, don't you?"

"Yes, sweetheart. You've convinced me. As you get older we'll have to figure out how you should use your talent."

"I don't want to use it, Daddy. I just like to talk to animals. And they love it when they find a human who can talk to them."

"All right, Sammie. We'll wait and see. Just remember, you start school next week and you have to keep your talent to yourself. Remember what happened in Alaska."

"Is that what it is Dad? A talent?"

He laughed. "That's as close as I can come to describing it, honey. Use it wisely."

"How will I know?"

"You'll have to decide yourself, like when you saved the school children from the rabid wolverine."

"They didn't appreciate it much, did they?"

"I'm sure they did. People are just scared sometimes when people are different than themselves. That's why you have to be careful."

"Alright, Dad. I'll try."

"That's all anyone can do, Sweetheart. Use your talent wisely and you'll have some wonderful adventures as you grow older."

Samantha smiled and patted Shafus on the head. The future beckoned like a bright light in the sky. How could she not have a wonderful time when she could talk to animals?

The End

The reason for the rather abrupt ending is that I plan on expanding Samantha's Talent into a full book intended for children and young adults, although I think almost anyone ought to be able to enjoy this story.

Also by Darrell Bain and published by LL-Publications

The hilarious tale of little Tonto, the dog who has to save the world from an accidental alien invasion!

"Tonto, a cross-eyed, ADHD affected little Weenie Dog with only one testicle is suddenly called upon to save the world from an alien invasion! Can he do the job? Well, perhaps, if a compulsively cursing alcoholic super-genius and his co-ed groupies combine forces with a cigar-chomping Italian from the pentagon and his air headed secretary. And of course they have to have help from Tonto's owners, who think politicians aren't much smarter than lizards.

"This is a science fiction novel so insane it only begins to make sense when it's discovered that the aliens had a part in Tonto's conception to begin with!"

Included in **BARK!** is the autobiography of Darrell's own quirky little dog, Tonto, the inspiration behind **BARK!**

Also by LL-Publications

2009 Eppie Award-winning novel for Best Horror;

PIT-STOP by Ben Larken

LAST CHANCE AT REDEMPTION FOR THE NEXT MILLION YEARS.

Welcome to the Pit-Stop Grill, a roadside attraction along Arizona's Route 66 where travelers kick up their feet while sipping a nice cup of joe. It's a cool oasis in an unforgiving desert landscape. It's also the last stop on the road to Hell.

When ten people find themselves inside the eerie diner, unable to get out or remember how they arrived, all they know is what their waitress, Holly, tells them: a bus is coming. It will take them the rest of the way to a destination of unspeakable horrors. Led by highway patrolman, Officer Scott Alders, the group of strangers unite with a common goal--escape. Each of them holds dark secrets, but personal demons are no match for the wraithlike bus driver who arrives bearing the nametag *RAMSEY*.

Driving an oily black bus with ghostly headlights and exhaust that smells of brimstone, Ramsey wastes no time picking them off one by one. As their number dwindles and the terror mounts, Scott Alders realizes it will take more than a police-issued sidearm to stop the evil that tracks them. But is there enough power in their battered spirits to combat a crimson-eyed driver with a schedule to keep? One thing is clear: you'll think twice before you make your next Pit-Stop.

"Ben Larken's **Pit-Stop** is a non-stop thrill ride from the beginning 'til the end. One of the best up-coming writers I have had the pleasure of reading in a long time. Right up there with King, Barker and Straub."
—*John Parker, Head: The Southern Horror Writers Association*

"**Pit-Stop** is an extraordinary horror/noir thriller. I can strongly recommend this book. It will shake your faith if you have one, make you wish you had faith otherwise."
—*Geoff Nelder, reviewer for Compulsive Reader and Café Doom*

The Hollows - Book 1: The Ticking by Ben Larken

1949
A young girl is traumatized when she witnesses a grisly murder in the forest behind her home.

1999
A loving wife disappears in the middle of the night, leaving no trace of her whereabouts.

2009
Former detective David Alders rents an apartment at a typical complex; a quiet unassuming place nestled in the outskirts of Fort Worth called The Hollows.

David is at a dead end after ten maddening years searching for his vanished wife. With mounting bills and a daughter on the verge of college, he makes the only logical choice: sell the family home, get back to work, and take a cheap apartment. His daughter, Melanie, is secretly thrilled about the change hoping it means a fresh start for their withering family.

But The Hollows has other plans...

As a new community welcomes the Alders into its midst, elusive figures watch from the periphery, waiting for their moment. On the first night, a grotesque, burnt man seizes Melanie in her bed, spewing insane ramblings before disappearing into the darkness. She struggles to convince her father what happened was real, but David has his own problems.

Like the fact that he has just woke up in the wrong day.

Welcome to a tour through the dark underbelly of the last half-century where invisible hands take you by force to the demons of your past. Where you can find terror, time travel, and murder—all for one low monthly rent.

Welcome to... THE HOLLOWS.

Pray that the lease agreement expires before you do.

The Great Right Hope, by Mark Jackman

"Even the best vampires need a good smack..."

In north-east England, a monster has arisen. A vampire beast is stalking the Yorkshire moors, mutilating and destroying everything in its path. The vampire elders realise that the Firmamentum has cast its shadow on the world once more–a phenomenon which happens every few millennia, where a human and a vampire are born ultimately powerful and destined to oppose each other...

Sid Tillsley is a forty-six year old benefit-fraudster from Middlesbrough. He's an overweight alcoholic, and also sexist, homophobic and a lazy git. But one thing sets him apart from his northern brethren; he can kill vampires with a single punch.

Suddenly, and very reluctantly, Sid finds himself the centre of human and vampire attention. Some want to kill him, but others believe him to be the Bellator; the one to fight the vampire beast.

ORDINARY WORLD by Tony McGuin

Murder isn't murder if it's served with fries...

"A modest proposal for the 21st century..."

This is the future.

Democratic institutions in the West have collapsed under the weight of the public's fear of terrorist attack. In uncertain times what people crave is the firm smack of fatherly dictatorship and the Church has stepped in to ensure a firm smack is exactly what the people get.

A world now betrothed to organized religion has nevertheless allowed big business to become even more debauched. GORDON A. GARGOYLE, owner of Recovered

Unwanted Meat Deals, (RUM Deals) UK, a manufacturer of reprocessed meat run-off, has secured a concession to exploit the virgin market of producing burgers made from aborted babies. As far as Gargoyle is concerned, the only thing Jonathan Swift lacked was a slogan and a jingle.

Can anybody stop this? Well, with the seemingly random interventions of two desperate friends, a child-smitten romantic, the world's most feeble (and ginger) terrorist, a cancer-ridden devil dog, a curious little blue car and a mysteriously knowing Pub landlord, somebody may already have. Mornings are hateful. Afternoons are quite pleasant. It's just another day in an Ordinary World.

No ordinary book, ORDINARY WORLD is a refined taste of exquisite satire which takes a stab at a near future world gone mad...

A HUMAN REACTION

by Peter Ashley

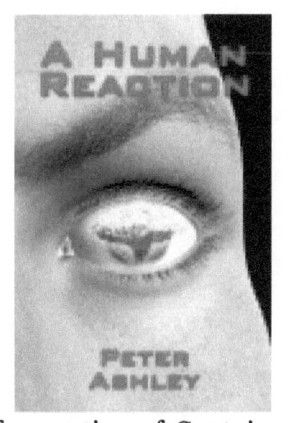

Earth is gripped in a devastating, post-apocalyptic final war that only one nation will be allowed to survive...

In his quest to bring a proud nation to its knees, Commander John Henson fails to destroy a seemingly insignificant enemy base, and in doing so is captured.

Lost: Commander John Henson, wanted for his lethal ability to obliterate the enemy compound of Fort Millawa, missing in action along with fellow soldier and lover, Salome.

Found: "Prisoner X" awakes to find himself a captive of Captain Rachel Dahan. He must now face what he has inadvertently found—a new perspective on the destructive conflict that has torn civilisation apart, and its impact on his very soul.

A Human Reaction finds a man suddenly no longer dedicated to his old life but struggling for a place in a new world.

**All books are available from
www.ll-publications.com,
Amazon, Barnes & Noble,
and all good retailers!**

www.ingramcontent.com/pod-product-compliance
Lightning Source LLC
Chambersburg PA
CBHW022100170626
46808CB00002B/515